Mentor to the Marquess

The Seductive Sleuths
Book 2

Melissa Kendall

ARE YOU SIGNED UP FOR DRAGONBLADE'S BLOG?

You'll get the latest news and information on exclusive giveaways, exclusive excerpts, coming releases, sales, free books, cover reveals and more.

Check out our complete list of authors, too!

No spam, no junk. That's a promise!

Sign Up Here

www.dragonbladepublishing.com

Dearest Reader;

Thank you for your support of a small press. At Dragonblade Publishing, we strive to bring you the highest quality Historical Romance from some of the best authors in the business. Without your support, there is no 'us', so we sincerely hope you adore these stories and find some new favorite authors along the way.

Happy Reading!

CEO, Dragonblade Publishing

Additional Dragonblade books by Author Melissa Kendall

The Seductive Sleuths Series
Companion to the Count (Book 1)
Mentor to the Marquess (Book 2)

Chapter One

ACCUSED MURDERESS IN LONDON. I must draw attention to the reappearance of Lady Olivia Allen in London, upon whom several suspicions have been piled. Of note, the death of her husband two years ago. I advise all men in want of a wife to take heed, lest you befall the same fate.

London, June 15, 1861

OLIVIA HEATHER, THE Countess Dowager Allen, slammed the newspaper onto the garden table, making the teacups rattle in their saucers. Not that anyone would notice. All the other tables on the terrace were empty, despite it being one of the few places where Mrs. Zephyr's guests could find shelter from the blazing sunlight.

"I assume the meeting with the editor did not go well," Olivia's friend Saffron Mayweather, the Viscountess Briarwood, said as she tucked a lock of black hair that had fallen out of her coiffure back into place. There was a slight roundness to her face, but the diagonal pleating of her lilac day gown hid all other signs of her pregnancy.

Olivia remembered how the editor of the *London Evening Standard* had sneered from across his desk. She put her hands in her lap and squeezed her fan so tight that the wood creaked. "I cannot expect assistance from that quarter."

All men had a price, but Mr. Ainsley could not be bought

with money, at least not by a woman. She might have tried to convince him to stop publishing the articles anyway, but she didn't trust him to keep his word even if she paid him a fortune. The scandal had made the *London Evening Standard* the most popular newspaper in town.

"What are you going to do?" Saffron asked. Her eyes glittered with the same excitement as they had several months prior, when Olivia had attempted to help her unmask the anonymous artist Ravenmore in an effort to locate Saffron's missing brother. That was before they'd learned Viscount Briarwood *was* Ravenmore, and Saffron's brother had died in the same boat accident that had killed the viscount's sister.

"As it happens, I did not come away from my meeting with the editor empty-handed," Olivia said. She removed a folded piece of paper from her pocket and slid it across the table. "I snatched this from his desk before he threw me out."

Saffron unfolded the paper and squinted as she brought it close to her face. "Remarkable. There is actually someone whose handwriting is worse than yours."

Olivia grabbed for the paper, but Saffron jerked away. "Yes, yes." She cleared her throat and read, "*Mr. Ainsley, Please ensure the attached article is printed in tomorrow's paper. Your usual fee is attached. Sincerely, Lowell.*" She flipped the paper over but did not read it aloud. Olivia was grateful. She had no desire to hear the vile accusations in her friend's voice.

Saffron handed the paper back. "I haven't seen the Marquess of Lowell in years. What reason would he have for attacking you?"

Olivia returned the letter to her pocket. "I wish I knew."

In the hours since learning his name, she had discovered exactly two facts about the marquess: his wife had died shortly after bearing a daughter, and the family had not been seen in society since.

A small part of her envied him. As much as she'd enjoyed her popularity before the articles, *Lady Allen* was nothing but a mask she'd crafted through two decades of careful observation from her husband's shadow. Her true self, the Olivia who held entire conversations without making eye contact and flapped her hands when she was excited, would never be accepted in society.

The Earl of Allen had made that lesson abundantly clear.

A high-pitched squeal drew her attention to the lawn, where a gaggle of children chased a tall woman in a pale-green day dress. The woman swished a wand through the air, forming hundreds of bubbles that floated above the shrieking children and vanished into the gently waving boughs of the trees above them.

"Is that Mrs. Gilly?" Saffron asked, gesturing to the woman. "I hardly recognize her without a book clutched in her arms."

Olivia smiled. "She was one of my first clients."

After two unsuccessful seasons, Seraphina's parents had begged Olivia to take the quiet, awkward girl under her wing. In a matter of weeks, Seraphina had wed Mr. Gilly, a textiles merchant, and all reports indicated their marriage was a happy one.

Olivia's smile fell. Since the articles had started, not a single mama had approached her to sponsor their daughter. Her schedule, once bustling with visits to modistes and milliners, had slowed to a crawl.

"I could ask my husband to speak to Lord Lowell," Saffron said, sliding her fork through a slice of lemon cake. She took a bite, then wrinkled her nose.

"Too sweet?" Olivia asked. She picked up a fork and speared the slice of strawberry from atop the cake. The surfeit of fresh fruit on display in the refreshment room was impressive but hardly a display of wealth. Strawberries were in season and therefore plentiful.

"Too sour." Saffron slid the plate across the table. "Leo can be properly intimidating. I am certain he could convince the marquess to cease his writing."

Olivia ate a piece of the "too sour" cake, giving herself a moment to come up with a response. She didn't want to insult her friend, but she wasn't interested in having another man solve her problem.

Ten years of marriage had taught her the importance of self-sufficiency.

The cake was sublime, with a coarse crumb that melted on her tongue and a layer of chopped strawberries in icing. She finished the entire piece, then set her fork down. "While I appreciate Lord Briarwood's physical prowess, I believe a more delicate hand is required." She tapped her finger on the newspaper. "The marquess might have more resources at his disposal, but I have yet to meet a gentleman who could turn away a woman in distress."

Once she discovered where he was hiding, she would don a heavy cloak and show up at his door at dawn with tears in her eyes. In the unlikely event he refused her, she would bring her burliest manservant to guarantee admittance. Then she would negotiate in a way only a woman could.

"Perhaps that will not be necessary," Saffron said. "Considering he just arrived."

Olivia whipped her neck around and followed her friend's gaze to the crowd gathered around an absolute mountain of a man in a charcoal suit standing at the bottom of the steps to the terrace. His black hair flowed down a square jaw into a thick beard and mustache liberally dusted with silver.

The way Lord Lowell tilted his head and clenched his hands into fists at his sides suggested a deep unease. Considering how long he had been a recluse, she was not surprised. She also found it difficult to re-don her Lady Allen mask after a significant amount of time away from society, as if her body had forgotten the movements.

She realized she was squeezing her fan again and forcibly relaxed her muscles. This was her chance to confront him. If her marriage had taught her anything, it was that men responded favorably to women who were willing to stroke their egos, among other things.

"That must be his daughter," Saffron said. "I haven't seen Constance since she was a babe."

Olivia wrenched her attention away from Lord Lowell. There was indeed a slip of a girl in a peach gown pressed to his side. The girl stepped forward and made a perfect curtsey before Mrs. Zephyr, who had cut her way through the crowd to greet the new arrivals. Their host, who was only a few years older than Saffron, all but bounced out of her frothy, pink gown as she greeted the marquess. Her words were lost amid the murmur of the crowd, but it was easy to guess what she was saying.

"*Oh, how utterly lovely, how wonderful to meet you,*" Olivia said in falsetto, as Mrs. Zephyr ran her white-gloved fingers through the loose, blonde curls at her nape. "*Please do admire this expensive, hideous gown. I chose it just for you, my lord.*"

Saffron snorted. "That's probably not even much of an exaggeration."

Lord Lowell's tense posture did not alter as Mrs. Zephyr held out a hand in a move clearly intended to pressure him into giving her his arm. Instead, he gave a sharp bow, then ascended the steps to the terrace with Constance at his side.

"Quite a cut," Saffron said. "Mrs. Zephyr does not look pleased."

Olivia was too busy watching Lord Lowell to care about their host's sensibilities. It could not have been more perfect. She would not have to arrange a private audience, because his path led directly to her table.

He reached the top of the steps, and his gaze met hers. Although she couldn't see his lips from beneath his wiry beard, the lines around his eyes suggested a smirk.

He stopped a respectable distance away and inclined his head. "Lady Allen." Then he turned to Saffron. "Miss Summersby. My mother sends her regards."

"It's Lady Briarwood now," Saffron said. "My aunt will be pleased to learn you have returned to town. How long will you be staying?"

"That is yet to be determined." He lowered his voice. "May we join your table? There is a matter I wish to discuss."

Gooseflesh pebbled Olivia's arms. His voice was so deep. She imagined his head between her thighs, his thick beard caressing her most sensitive areas, his rumbling baritone vibrating her flesh. The sheer size of him suggested she would not come away unsatisfied.

What am I thinking?

The man was a blackguard. He had ruined her life. She should have been thinking of ways to bend him to her will, not imagining them in bed together. No matter how attractive she found him.

The silence stretched. Saffron coughed delicately into her napkin.

Olivia straightened her shoulders. "Of course. We would welcome your company."

Before she had even finished speaking, he was pulling out a chair for his daughter, as if the thought of her refusing him, a marquess, had never entered his mind. It was true, but that didn't dampen her anger in the slightest.

At least he waited for his daughter to sit before doing the same.

"You should apologize for our rudeness, Father," Lady Constance said. "It was not appropriate to impose upon Lady Allen's time without first requesting an introduction."

Lady Constance was as much a surprise as her father. Olivia recognized the careful hand of a governess who was plentiful with both correction and praise, rather than punishing every perceived slight. The girl could not be older than nineteen, yet she displayed the poise of a mature woman.

The footman returned with two other servants. One placed a three-tiered stand of fruit-laden cakes on their table, a second set down four glasses of lemonade, and a third provided them with additional plates.

"No need to apologize," Olivia said. "Our actions will have

convinced the watchers below that we are of long acquaintance. I see no reason to correct anyone of that notion."

Settling their dispute would be awkward enough without Mrs. Zephyr hovering over them.

Lord Lowell's shoulders sank. "Then you have surmised my intent. Excellent. I fear I have spoken to, and been rejected by, every matron in London."

"You have… what?" The conversation wasn't heading in the direction she'd expected. "Surely, there is a more pressing matter for us to discuss."

He frowned. "What might that be?"

The man was either obtuse or frustrating her on purpose. "What do you want from me, Lord Lowell?"

He blinked several times before shaking his head. "As you wish, I will be direct. I desire your services as a matchmaker."

Saffron paused her fork midway to her mouth. "You cannot be serious."

Olivia kicked her friend's shin. She was beginning to understand his ploy. He had soured her reputation, driving all other mamas away, to force her to accept his daughter. He needn't have bothered. She would not have rejected the daughter of a marquess, even if her schedule had been packed.

Lord Lowell's strategy would have met with her former husband's approval. The Earl of Allen had derived much enjoyment from manipulating and tormenting others.

She throttled back her temper. "You want me to find a husband for your daughter?"

His frown returned. "If that is acceptable. I understand your services are in high demand."

Saffron made a choking sound that sounded suspiciously like a laugh.

Olivia's jaw ached. How dare he make light of her misfortune? He was well aware her services were *not* in high demand, and it was his fault. First, he had accused her of murdering her late husband, then compounded the indignity by implying she was seeking another man to marry and repeat the crime.

"I can fit her into my schedule," she said through clenched teeth. Then, to distract herself from committing an act that would wipe the ridiculous look of relief from his face, she turned her attention to his daughter. "Do you wish for a gentle introduction to society?"

Lady Constance shook her head, making the flowers tucked into her curls bounce. "I would prefer to *leap in*." She plucked a strawberry from the top of a piece of cake on the bottom tier of the stand and popped it in her mouth.

"Constance," Lord Lowell said in a long-suffering tone.

The girl picked up the strawberry-less cake and placed it on her plate. "Sorry."

The interaction between them was both amusing and surprising.

Olivia was used to demanding mamas but had never met a father or guardian who had any interest in his daughter's future husband beyond the usual contractual matters.

Proper title and breeding. Sufficient funds to support a wife. Ideally, property.

Coincidentally, those were the same criteria most managing mamas cared about.

"You should know I do not promise a match," she said. "Nor will I agree to trap a man."

She'd seen far too many women resort to such tactics, arranging compromising situations to force a man's hand. Somehow, they never considered the husband they caught would hold significant power over his new wife.

Olivia knew all too well how it felt to be in such a position.

"I wouldn't expect you to," Lord Lowell said. He glanced at Saffron, then blurted out, "Love. That is the condition all other matrons have refused. I will allow nothing less than a love match for my daughter."

Olivia was rendered speechless. She thought it was another joke, but he wasn't laughing.

Saffron stuffed a small cake into her mouth, her eyes wide.

"I have arranged dozens of matches, my lord," Olivia said, choosing her words with care. "I can assure you; love does not simply spark into existence the way one lights a match."

She had learned that lesson the hard way. If it were not for her youthful folly, she might have saved herself ten years of misery. As far as she was concerned, only children believed in love. She glanced at Constance, who was staring at her plate with a small smile on her face, seemingly uninterested in the conversation they were having about her future. That was curious. In Olivia's experience, most girls on the cusp of their debut struggled to contain their excitement, no matter how strict their upbringing. But how the girl felt about marriage was of little consequence, as her father would make the most important decisions on her behalf.

Olivia turned her attention back to Lord Lowell. "You might find compatibility is a better foundation for a marriage."

He opened his mouth to reply but was interrupted by Mrs. Zephyr rushing across the terrace toward them. When she reached them, she fluffed her voluminous skirts. "Lord Lowell, I thought I would give you a tour of the grounds. You and your lovely daughter. There are several eligible young men I could introduce her to."

Olivia hissed in a breath. Mrs. Zephyr was trying to usurp her position, likely in an attempt to endear herself to the wealthy and widowed marquess.

"I'm afraid Lord Lowell and Lady Constance are presently engaged," Olivia said. "We were just discussing the particulars of Lady Constance's debut, under my sponsorship."

Mrs. Zephyr drew herself up. "Lord Lowell, you are newly returned to London. I insist you do not make such an important decision so rashly."

Olivia slid her chair back at the same time as Saffron, but Lord Lowell beat them both to his feet.

"I find myself unimpressed with the fare," he said. "Lady

Allen, I would be pleased if you would call upon us tomorrow morning. Constance, let us proceed to our next engagement at the Duke of Haversham's estate."

"The wild duke?" Mrs. Zephyr staggered back a step. "I-I shall not keep you, my lord. Please, give the duke my regards." Then she whirled back down the stairs.

Far from being cowed by Mrs. Zephyr's outburst, Olivia felt invigorated in a way she hadn't in weeks. Society expected her to bow down before the rumors and descend the social hierarchy. She would show them she would not bend to mere gossip. As furious as she was with the marquess for being the cause of her misfortune, accepting his daughter as her client would allow her to grow closer to him and make him pay for what he had done. Lord Lowell's daughter would find a love match if it was the last thing she did.

Chapter Two

T HELLUSSON VAITH, MARQUESS of Lowell, stretched out in his chair and held the smoke from his cigar in his mouth. He loved the rich, peppery taste of American tobacco, even though his mother's lips pursed whenever she smelled it.

"Are you sure about this, Thel?" his brother Felix asked as he lounged his lanky frame in a leather chaise. His curly, black hair was even more unruly than usual, like a topiary that had yet to be pruned. He held a cigar in one hand and with the other reached into the front pocket of his single-breasted black frock coat to remove a box of matches, which he shook. A rattling came from inside. He pushed the box open, removed a match, and lit his cigar.

The hazy room was filled with books stacked on shelves from the floor to the ceiling. A fire roared in the hearth beneath a portrait of his parents smiling indulgently upon them. The story of that portrait was one his mother had told him many times. His father had met his future wife at a garden party, recognized her as his true love, and proposed marriage in a matter of days.

"She is the one," Thel said, releasing the smoke. That was all he should have needed to say. His brothers knew that once he made up his mind, he rarely changed it. That was how they'd managed to live together for so long, half a dozen adults and almost as many children under one roof. Other families would have descended into quarrels after days of such cohabitation, but family counted on him to resolve any such problems.

"It's not too late to select an appropriate husband for her," Felix said. He ran his thumb and forefinger over his wiry mustache. "I know several eligible gentlemen in possession of valuable business assets who would be amenable to a match."

"I am not using Constance as a bartering tool."

"Choose another matchmaker, then," Felix said. "There are scandals swirling around that woman." He slid the newspaper that sat on the table between them toward Thel.

Thel slid it back. "Rumors are not fact. Do you not remember what they said about me after Marguerite died?"

The scandal rags had first accused him of causing his wife's illness by allowing her to venture into the poor areas of the city to do her charity work, then had attributed his withdrawal from society as proof of their claims. As far as he was concerned, the newspapers, especially the *London Evening Standard*, printed more lies than truth.

Felix might have disapproved of his choice, but Lady Allen was the only matchmaker he had approached who had been willing to abide by his requirement that Constance find a husband who would complete her life as surely as his mother had completed his father's and Marguerite had completed his own.

A familiar ache started in his chest. He fondly remembered the brief kisses he'd shared with his wife in the drawing room before receiving guests. The gentle caressing of hands while walking in the park. The soft stroke of a hand along a cheek after finishing dinner.

His only regret was that those moments had been rare because he had devoted most of his time to his own selfish interests: reading, writing, and collecting antique manuscripts. It had taken his wife's illness and eventual death for him to realize how painful loneliness could be. To avoid ever experiencing that aching emptiness and loss of purpose again, he'd convinced his parents to come live with him and Constance part of the year. Then Felix had married and the new couple had agreed to join them year-round at the marquess's estate—a feat which had required weeks of negotiation with each member of his family. Their youngest brother had followed, living with the family at Thel's whenever he wasn't abroad or in London. If everything went according to plan, Constance's future husband would join them as well.

"My decision is final," Thel said. "Constance deserves a chance at love."

Felix sighed. "You are too innocent, brother. It clouds your judgment. If you would only find a courtesan…"

They had revisited this dispute so many times that Thel knew exactly what Felix would say next.

"Father expects you to remarry and produce an heir. What if you are unable to satisfy your future wife?"

It was the only argument Thel admitted held some weight. Their father had made his wishes regarding succession clear. It didn't matter that Thel had two brothers, one of whom had already sired sons. The previous four dukes had been eldest sons of eldest sons and their father was determined not to break the tradition. At some point, Thel would become a duke, and yet at five-and-forty, he had only ever bedded one woman. He had assured his family he would remarry after Constance was wed, but he did not expect that he would ever experience what he had with Marguerite again.

He had found, and lost, his true love.

Felix pushed out of the chair and walked across to the bookshelves. "If you won't indulge yourself physically"—he slid his finger along the leather spines—"then at least educate yourself so you know what you are missing." He pulled out a book and set it on the table between them.

Thel knew exactly what it was, having read every book in the library. He tried to tell his brother, but the words stuck in his throat. Felix would call him a hypocrite if he knew his brother had studied books of pleasure.

"Peruse this, and if it sparks passion in you, then there are several courtesans I could recommend." Felix set the stub of his cigar on the ashtray and sauntered out of the room.

As the door thumped shut, Thel slid his hand over the soft, leather cover of the book, fingering the letters tooled into the fabric. He didn't need to open it to have images flow into his mind, one after another. Each page held a detailed illustration of a nude man and woman—or sometimes multiple men and women—contorted together in increasingly complicated positions. He had given a copy to Marguerite as a birthday gift, but she had fallen ill before they'd had a chance to try any of the techniques.

He stood and returned the book to its place on the shelf, then walked along the shelves until he found a thinner book, the first volume in a set of three, its spine lovingly worn. He cradled it against his chest. Felix would laugh uproariously if he learned about Thel's favorite reading material. As close as they were, his younger brothers modeled themselves around his stern but loving father.

Thel, on the other hand, was more like their mother. He remembered sitting in her lap as a young boy, listening to her read. Sometimes his father would join them, and they would curl up on the bed and enjoy each other's company.

That was a family. An environment of love, where any word spoken in anger was immediately chased away by an apology. His brothers could pursue loveless futures for their children if they desired, but he would not let them force Constance down the same path.

He took a final draw of his cigar, then set it on the ashtray. He didn't bother closing the flume to the furnace, where the fire crackled and popped in the hearth. The servants would take care of it, in addition to cleaning the ash and restocking the pile of wood and matches.

He left the room and entered a long hallway. Sunlight shone through the foggy, glass windows and formed dots of light on the walls. When he reached his daughter's room, he knocked softly. A short, bespectacled woman with silver-blonde hair tied in a tight bun opened the door. Constance's governess and now lady's maid, Mrs. Quill, who had once been his mother's favorite modiste. When Mrs. Quill's hands had become knobby with time spent hunched over fabric, his mother had offered the woman a position in their household.

"My lord," Mrs. Quill said. The tightness around her pale-blue eyes smoothed out. She stepped away and opened the door wide, revealing Constance sitting at her dressing table.

Mrs. Quill picked up a wicker basket full of wool. "Summon me when you wish to sleep, my lady."

As the lady's maid closed the door, Constance dove toward her bed. She lifted a pillow and withdrew a blue, leather book, identical to the one he held in his hands.

He eyed the slip of paper tucked in the book. "Have you read ahead?"

She plucked the bookmark free. "Of course not. Shall we continue at chapter…eight?"

"Six," Thel said as he sat on the chair by the fire and cracked open his copy of *Lady Audley's Secret*. In moments, he was swept away by George Talboys's grief upon learning of his wife's death. It reminded him of the nights he'd spent alone in his room after Marguerite's funeral. A lump formed in his throat. He might have followed his wife into death if it had not been for the promise she had extracted out of him, that he would care for their daughter until she wed.

He finished the chapter, set it down, and waited. It was not long before Constance sighed and clutched the book to her chest.

"It's so romantic," she said. "I cannot wait to find a man who loves me as much as George loved Helen."

"That is why we engaged Lady Allen. We will not rest until you have a George of your own."

She scooted to the edge of her bed and tugged at a strand of her hair, a sure sign she was troubled.

He crossed the room and put his hands on his daughter's shoulders. "What's wrong?"

"If George had found another woman to be his wife, he might not have been exiled by his family." Her lower lip trembled. "What if I fall in love with a commoner?"

Rather than placate her with assurances that had no real merit, he leaned back and considered. What would he do if his daughter's choice of husband was someone the rest of the family could not accept?

He knew what Marguerite would have done. She would have supported Constance, even if that meant they were expelled from society. Unfortunately, he was not so brave. He had spent a significant portion of his life bringing his family together. The moment they turned on each other, the harmony he had worked so hard to achieve would dissolve, and he'd end up alone once again.

"We would find a solution," he said. "One that would not involve shipping you to Australia."

It was the best he could come up with, and it seemed to satisfy his daughter, but as he said goodnight, he resolved that the next book they read would be one that would not raise such uncomfortable questions.

Chapter Three

LADY OLIVIA ALLEN STAKES HER CLAIM. I have become aware of a close acquaintance between the Countess Dowager Allen and Marquess of Lowell. It should be cautioned that this is not yet cause to celebrate, for the woman's promiscuous nature is well-known. The marquess might yet prove too pedestrian for Lady Allen's tastes.

O LIVIA CRUMPLED THE newspaper into a ball, dropped it onto the sticky floor of the carriage, and crushed it beneath the heel of her blue, satin slipper. She should not have been surprised that Lord Lowell had not stopped the articles, despite their deal. The man was a better actor than any she had ever seen on stage. He maintained a careful innocence when she was in his presence, then returned to cruelty the moment she left his sight.

Or perhaps she was attributing too much intelligence to her enemy. This wasn't a man who understood how to manipulate, but one who used whatever clumsy tool was at his disposal to achieve his goal.

The carriage rattled to a stop, and a servant dressed in green-and-gold livery opened her door. She took his hand and ascended the pristine steps leading to a towering house. It was three stories tall with a brick façade covered in winding ivy and dormers over the three windows on the top level. A ducal residence. She had almost forgotten that Lord Lowell was heir to a dukedom.

A bead of sweat dripped down her chin. It was unfortunate that the nature of her visit required tighter adherence to formality, or she would have worn something lighter than her pale-blue linen day dress. The garment accentuated her figure, but the full-length sleeves clasped her in a tight embrace and the jet beads decorating her hat hung like a noose about to drop around her neck.

She fluffed her skirts and followed the footman up the steps. The closer she got, the more she became aware of sound filtering through the door: the murmur of many voices speaking, the shrill cry of children's laughter, the patter of running feet. It was a remarkable amount of noise, and she hoped it didn't mean she was about to interrupt an event, even though Lord Lowell had explicitly invited her the previous afternoon.

The footman reached the top of the stairs before her and drew the door open, causing her to stop short.

If she had the wherewithal to design an entryway that perfectly suited her tastes, it would be very similar to what lay before her. An enormous, gold chandelier hung above white, marble floors that led to a grand staircase carpeted in a pattern of silver stars on red. There were no cracked tiles or mildewy corners. Every inch of space was spotless, a difficult feat with so many people living under one roof.

And there were people, so many bodies bustling about, that her fears of being an inopportune caller returned. When no butler or housekeeper appeared to greet her, she nearly turned on her heel. Instead, she straightened her shoulders and strode into the chaos.

The appearance of Lady Allen always attracted attention—eventually.

She had barely passed the threshold when a group of four brown-haired children appeared out of nowhere, running toward her with their arms outstretched. She stood rooted to the spot, a rock jutting out of the ocean, and let them wash over her. They pressed their sticky hands to her dress and began speaking all at once.

"You're the most beautiful lady I've ever seen," a rosy-cheeked child said. "My name's Bennett. What's yours?"

"Connie's gowns aren't as pretty as yours," a child with the same dark eyes as Lord Lowell asked. "Go away, Bennett. I got to her first, and I'm older than you."

With their faces turned toward her, their bodies pressed into her skirt, it was easy to imagine they were her own.

"One at a time, darlings," she said. She cupped the backs of their heads, running her fingers through their feather-soft hair. She had a special place in her heart for children. They were impossibly curious. She remembered standing in front of her mirror in her room with one of her mother's dresses held to her thin body, imagining twirling around with a handsome prince.

Unfortunately, it hadn't been a prince who had caught her interest, but a villain disguised as an earl.

"Are you going to come live with us?" a third child, who couldn't have been more than six, asked. She gave a gap-toothed smile. "There's lots of space. The house is *thiiis* big." She stretched her arms wide.

"I wish I could, darling," she said. "I would be your fairy godmother, conjuring gowns out of spider silk and sunbeams." She mimed waving a wand over their heads and chanted nonsense words that made them giggle.

"You could stay in the room beside mine," Bennett said. "I can show you!"

"Children," Lord Lowell said.

The clipped word jolted her back to reality and brought the young ones to attention. They detached from her skirt and made pretty bows or curtseys, then formed a line in front of the grand staircase.

She was both relieved and disappointed to see them go. The former because they were a painful reminder of a life she had always wanted, and the latter because it had been years since she'd felt so much like the woman she'd been before the earl had routed every ounce of whimsy from her soul.

"I apologize," Lord Lowell said. "They are most active in the afternoon."

"I adore children," she said. Then she took his offered arm because Lady Allen was always happy to be next to a handsome man, even as Olivia's skin pebbled at the close contact.

It doesn't matter how attractive he is. He ruined your reputation.

"Did you have plans for the day?" he asked.

His question reminded her of the purpose of her visit. He was not a normal client, but a man who had accused her of murder.

"I thought I could accompany your daughter to my modiste this afternoon."

There were many shops she could take the girl to, ladies who owed her favors, but she would begin with the one with whom she had the longest acquaintance. Madame Julian, originally from Paris, had set up shop in London five summers past and had outfitted Olivia with several of her favorite gowns.

There would be no awkward incidents for Lady Constance in her first season, unlike how it had been for poor Miss Trellow, whose breasts had popped out of her bodice during her first ball because of her mother's insistence upon the girl wearing a dress that dipped so low, it barely covered her nipples.

"Constance will be pleased," Lord Lowell said. He squeezed her fingers and led her toward the stairs. "Did you come to any difficulty on the way here?"

She looked at him askance. "No. Why do you ask?"

He stopped. "I saw the newspaper this morning. The articles are getting bolder."

A veiled threat? The man already had her commitment, her binding word. What else did he want from her?

She straightened her back. "You should know that I will not allow rumors to disrupt my plans."

"I would expect nothing less."

She had to bite the inside of her cheek to stop a sharp retort from bursting free. His complete lack of shame was infuriating, but she was not so impolite that she would insult him in front of his family and servants.

He began walking again, to her relief. When he looked at her, her wits scattered, making it difficult to hold on to her carefully constructed mask.

Lady Allen was capable of dancing circles around Lord Lowell and his many charms.

Olivia was not.

Chapter Four

THEL FOUND IT difficult to release Lady Allen's hand when they reached the top of the stairs. He wanted to clutch her close and chase away the coldness that had settled over her when he'd mentioned the newspaper. It had felt as if she were angry with him, although he wasn't sure what he'd done to upset her. Perhaps it was the articles.

He had considered using his resources to track the source of the articles down, but Lady Allen had not requested his assistance, and he would not offend her by getting involved without her consent. If she required his help, she would ask for it.

He had never met a woman who was more in control of herself, as if she could command the dark locks coiled atop her head to remain perfectly in place, despite the breeze from the open windows.

An image flashed into his mind of her on her hands and knees on his bed, her rear presented for his enjoyment, a silky, black waterfall spilling over her shoulders.

He mentally shook himself. His personal desires were irrelevant. Ensuring Constance found a loving husband was his highest priority. He had promised Marguerite.

When they reached Constance's room, he knocked. When no one answered, he turned the doorknob and eased the door open.

Constance sat at her writing desk, bent over a sheet of paper. She wore a bright-yellow tea gown that faded to a deep green at the hem. The color suited her sunny personality, and he made a mental note to thank Mrs. Quill for choosing it for her first day with her sponsor.

The door let out a creak, and Constance met his gaze in the mirror. She jolted upright. "Father!"

She looked so startled that he felt a twinge of guilt for interrupting, but she hurriedly returned her writing implements to their proper locations and stood. "Good morning, Father. Good morning, Lady Allen."

Olivia stepped closer. "If we are to be working together, we do not need to observe such formalities."

Constance pursed her lips. "You may call me by my Christian name, but as you are my sponsor, I should continue to refer to you as 'Lady Allen.'"

"If that is your wish," Lady Allen said, although it was clear from the crinkling around her eyes that she was holding back a smile. "Now, tell me, what is the name of the Duke of Wintermoor's eldest son?"

Constance hesitated a beat before replying, "Lord Adam. He has two sisters, Lady Deirdre and Lady Lilian."

Lady Allen nodded. "Excellent. What fare would you serve for an afternoon tea with Lord Adam and his sisters?"

"Sandwiches and tea or coffee, but not wine or beer."

"Entertainment?"

"Lady Lilian has a wonderful singing voice, and Lady Deirdre is very skilled at the pianoforte." She grinned. "I prefer to take my afternoon tea outdoors, if the weather is fair."

Thel strolled to his usual seat by the fireplace as Lady Allen tested his daughter's knowledge. She would find no deficits there. He had hired the best tutors and overseen her education himself. He would have proceeded with presenting her to society as well, if not for the fact that Felix's wife shared Felix's views regarding arranged marriages, and his mother's poor constitution meant she rarely ventured into London.

Lady Allen walked around the room as she fired off more

questions, giving him the chance to admire her from different angles. Her large, green eyes, framed by thick lashes. The soft curls at her nape. Her tall frame that would fit snugly against him, as very few women would. God could not have presented him with a better woman to test his resolve.

"Uncle," a soft voice said.

The room fell to a hush.

His youngest niece, Alanna, stood in the doorway, a pink blanket dragging along the floor. Behind her, Constance and Lady Allen watched in very different manners. Constance's scowl reminded him of the need for a discussion about boundaries with the other children. Lady Allen, however, clenched one hand at her waist and clutched a bedpost on Constance's bed with the other.

Alanna crossed the room and tugged on his trousers. "Want up."

He ruffled her black curls. "Trying to avoid naptime again?"

He knew better than to give her what she wanted. The head nanny had made it abundantly clear what the consequences were for the children missing their afternoon nap.

Alanna screwed up her tiny face and thrashed her blanket. "Up!"

A strangled cry came from Lady Allen, and then she knelt in front of his niece with her arms open. The powerful expression of yearning on her face left him speechless. Gone was the cold, sharp-tongued woman he'd bantered with on the stairs. The difference was striking and for a fleeting moment, he felt what he thought she was feeling, a familiar loneliness so sharp, it cut him up inside. He reached for her before he realized what he was doing, drawn to her pain, unable to stand the thought of her hurting.

Alanna shuffled back and shook her head.

"Come here, darling," Lady Allen said in a tremulous tone.

The sound of quickly approaching footfalls came from the hallway, and then the nanny said, "Has anyone seen a young girl up past her naptime?"

His niece stuck her thumb in her mouth and exited the room as fast as her little legs could carry her.

"How many dresses will I need?" Constance asked loudly.

Lady Allen straightened. "An excellent question. You must have evening gowns, of course, and at least one costume. Several afternoon dresses…"

He leaned back, stunned by the strength of emotion he'd felt. There was something about Lady Allen that reminded him so much of Marguerite. Not the cool, confident woman she portrayed to society, but the woman whose face had softened when his nieces and nephews had tugged at her skirt. It made him wonder why she had never had children of her own. She had certainly been married long enough, although to a much older man.

As he crossed his legs, something jabbed him in the thigh. He reached behind a cushion and withdrew a crumpled sheet of vellum. When he unfolded it and saw it was addressed to Constance, his first instinct was to place it back where he had found it. Then he skimmed a line that made him go cold.

He slipped the paper into his pocket and took his leave of the room. When he was back in his office, with the door locked, he spread the letter onto his desk and read it from the beginning. His stomach dropped with each word, and by the time he'd reached the end, his suspicions were confirmed.

He did not need to search out the person attacking Lady Allen in the newspaper because the source of the articles was living under his roof.

It was his own daughter.

Chapter Five

Dear Lord Lowell,

I must request an additional two hundred pounds to publish the article that you requested. If you do not respond, I believe Lady Allen would be amenable to a deal regarding your identity. I await your correspondence via the usual method.

Sincerely, Mr. Ainsley

O LIVIA SAT INSIDE the rocking carriage across from Constance and thanked God for her luck. The girl was bright, charming, and well-educated. Her family's wealth alone would attract a horde of suitors. She need only to guide the girl through encounters with suitable men and let youthful passion take hold.

If only Constance's father were so easy to manage.

Some of his actions had obvious intent, the smoldering looks, the gentle brush of his fingers along her back, the quirk of an eyebrow in response to a suggestive comment. She kept waiting for the bastard to pull her into a room and proposition her, but it never happened.

Perhaps that was for the best. Physical attraction aside, she doubted she could put aside her anger for long enough to appease whatever vile desires he possessed.

What she should have done was extract a promise that he would retract the statements in the articles when Constance was wed. But every time they were alone, she mooned over him like a girl in her first season. That could not continue. When she did not treat him as a threat, it was too easy to let down her guard and simply become Olivia.

Distractible, disastrous Olivia, who'd yearned for motherhood and had chosen a husband based on the fleeting whims of her heart rather than sense.

She wished she could go back and scream at that innocent girl to run as fast as she could.

The sound of the carriage rattling to a stop pulled her out of her thoughts.

Constance jerked her head around. "Have we arrived already?"

"Should I ask the driver to circle the block until you are ready?"

Constance flushed but was spared having to respond by their driver opening the door.

The thump of horse hooves on well-packed earth surrounded them, accompanied by the occasional whinny. Street urchins in brown caps darted through the crowd, offering newspapers for sale while slipping their small hands into the pockets of the unwary.

Olivia hustled her charge toward a windowless, brick building nestled between a milliner's and a general shop. She opened the door, and they stepped into a room that was filled with bolts of colored fabric stacked in cubbies along the walls from floor to ceiling. Dress forms wearing half-completed gowns hung from the ceiling above long tables like ghosts.

Constance flitted around the shop, exclaiming her pleasure in soft gasps and sighs. Olivia waited for her to settle and then joined her beside a section of floral prints.

"This is so lovely," Constance said, touching the frayed edge of a length of bronze muslin.

Olivia held it up. "What would you pair it with?"

"Cream or black," Constance said. She walked over to another row and tapped a gray paisley silk. "This one for the overskirt, the other for the gown. Trimmed in black or silver lace."

Olivia pictured the dress in her mind and nodded. "You have an excellent eye for fashion."

Constance grinned. "Aunt Celina says that, too. I sometimes help her choose her attire for events. She is fond of gold chiffon and Chantilly lace."

Olivia wondered what it must have been like growing up in a house full of love and life, where there was always a family member or caring servant to carry a sleepy child to bed and the dinner table was crowded with plates. Her early years had been desolate by comparison. There had been occasional events that had drawn them into the village, and a string of strict governesses, but otherwise, she'd occupied her childhood alone.

And most of her adulthood, for that matter.

The loneliest years of her life had been the ones she'd spent at her husband's side. Only as she'd grown older had she realized the earl had not been afflicted with an overabundance of affection, but possession. Any attempts she'd made to grant herself a moment of peace had been met with reprimands and rambling lectures on the importance of loyalty to one's husband.

What she would not give to strike the accursed man from her past.

She forcibly thrust her thoughts of her former husband away and flipped through a book of fashion plates as they waited for Madame Julian. That the modiste had left them on their own for so long was odd. The woman must have been busy. Still, the pounding in her chest increased with every passing minute.

She ran her finger over a sketch of a shepherdess costume. The square-cut bodice and full skirt were turquoise, with strips of white inlaid with pink roses. The three-quarter-length sleeves with double-layered cuffs were reminiscent of the French court gowns her grandmother had once owned. She coveted it immediately, although she had not attended a fancy-dress party in months. Perhaps she would commission it for herself, along with Constance's new wardrobe.

Once the girl was wed, the articles stopped, and her reputation restored, she would host a grand ball. It would be the perfect end to the season, an event celebrating her jubilant return to matchmaking. She would have so many candidates thrust upon her by eager mamas that her schedule would be booked for months.

She closed the book as a door thudded and Madame Julian stepped out of the darkness. Her black hair was held back from her face by a complicated arrangement of braids, and her rouged lips were turned down in a frown. Unlike during the previous times Olivia had visited, the modiste did not greet her with an explosion of rapid French but dipped her sharp chin while sliding a long strip of paper between her fingers.

"Lady Allen," the woman said, without meeting her gaze. "I apologize, but I cannot assist you. I am busy."

"Busy?"

Madame Julian had never turned her away. Without Olivia's patronage, she might never have left the unfashionable district where she had first set up shop.

Then Olivia spotted the newspaper laid out on the long table, beside a pile of fabric scraps.

"Madame, I cannot." The woman's large eyes watered. "My business. I cannot assist you. You must ask another." She rushed off, leaving Olivia standing beside an open-mouthed Constance.

"What was that?" Constance asked.

At least there were no other patrons in the shop to see what had happened. There would be no firsthand accounts of her embarrassment.

"A minor complication," Olivia said, forcing out each word. But as she drew Constance back to the waiting carriage, she could not help but wonder if Madame Julian would not help them, then who would?

Chapter Six

"**H**OW MUCH LONGER are you going to engage that woman?" Felix asked.

Thel speared a piece of charred beef from his plate and stuck it in his mouth as an excuse not to answer. His brother had been nettling him since Olivia and Constance had left. It would not usually have been a problem, except that he was unsure of his own feelings toward the woman.

That he desired her was obvious but did not explain why seeing her in distress made his chest ache, and why reaching for her seemed like the most natural thing in the world.

Perhaps it was only that she had surprised him. The gentle, soft-spoken lady who had opened her arms for Alanna was entirely different from the confident woman who had put Mrs. Zephyr in her place.

"If you continue to associate with her, how long until society turns on all of us?" his brother asked from across the table. "You must dismiss the wretched woman at once."

Elijah, their youngest brother, grimaced. Unlike Thel and Felix, the sharp planes of Elijah's face were clean shaven, and he kept his dark-brown hair short. At three-and-twenty, he was the only one of them who was still a never-married, confirmed bachelor, despite their mother's pestering.

"The articles *are* rather concerning," Felix's wife, Celina, said. She dabbed her lips with a black, silk handkerchief, despite having consumed no more than a bite of every plate that had been placed before her. He had no idea how she maintained her fashionably curvy figure without the appearance of an appetite.

"Quite right," Felix said. He pinned Thel with a glare. "What would Father think, if he knew a woman of such dubious reputation was in close contact with his granddaughter?"

Thel didn't want to think about the articles. He should have confronted his daughter before she'd left with Lady Allen, but he had been too set on finding another meaning in the letter that he had missed. It made little sense that Constance was attacking Lady Allen. First, the articles had started weeks before they had met her. Second, if Constance held some grudge against Lady Allen, why had she not balked when he had suggested engaging her services?

Elijah put his hand on Felix's shoulder. "Thel has made his decision. We must respect it."

Felix scoffed. "It was *his decision* not to marry Constance to an appropriate man, and now she is in the care of a woman accused of murder. We will be lucky if she survives the season with her reputation intact." He swung his arm around, tipping over his wife's glass and spilling wine onto her lap.

She shrieked as servants rushed to clear up the mess.

Felix continued, undeterred despite the flurry of activity around him. "She should have been matched as soon as her breasts began to bud. Men will be trying to get under her skirts—"

Thel pushed back from the table. "Enough!"

Felix quieted, but the resentment on his face was clear.

"I will not speak of this again." Thel swept his gaze down the table and made eye contact with each person present. "Constance will marry a man of her choosing. If we disapprove of her selection, then we will deal with that when the time comes. But you will not continue to question my decisions. Father has made it clear that as heir, I am the head of this house while he's away."

One by one, they looked down. Everyone except Felix.

"You don't deserve to be the heir," his brother whispered.

Then he stumbled out of his chair and down the hallway. His wife hurried after him, leaving a trail of red droplets in her wake.

"Excuse me, everyone, but I believe I have lost my appetite," Thel said before charging out of the dining room.

He did not want his family to see how badly Felix had rattled him. It would only upset the balance of harmony in the house when it was more important than ever for them to support one another. Part of him wondered if he had made a mistake not finding a husband for Constance earlier. As much as he wanted her to experience the love he had, he feared Felix would not easily give up his campaign to see her wed to a man of his choice. Whether Felix's determination was due to a desire to see his niece matched to an appropriate man, or something else, Thel didn't know, and he was not confident Felix would answer him if he asked.

When he was back in his office and behind his desk, he withdrew a leatherbound notebook and a pen. He was too angry to read, but his high emotions could be put to another use. The latest chapters of *Lady Audley's Secret* were unsatisfactory. He wanted to explore an alternative storyline where the main character's wife joined him when he left for Australia to prospect for gold. It would have been better for the couple to stay in England with the rest of their extended family, but he could not think of a way to accomplish that without venturing into the realm of fantasy.

He dipped his pen in the ink and began writing furiously. Images appeared in his head one by one, painted in wide strokes like a watercolor. With each line, a bit of anger drained out of him until he was left exhausted.

Perhaps Felix was right about his celibacy. His attraction to Lady Allen was a distraction. He would not betray Marguerite by involving his heart, but—if Lady Allen was amenable—a physical affair would allow him to slake his lust and ensure his skills in the bedroom were up to snuff. He was unsure what he could offer in exchange, but he had no doubt she would make her desires known.

If she did not demand reparations the moment he told her what he had found in Constance's room.

"There you are."

He slapped his notebook closed. Elijah stood in the open door, a cigar between his lips.

"Felix is furious," Elijah said as he sauntered into the room. "You know how he is, always acting like he's the heir. Like he has authority over the rest of us. Without Father here to set him right, he probably thinks he'll get away with it. I suspect he intended to use Constance in one of his business deals. You should not have engaged Lady Allen."

Thel didn't have the energy to remind his brother of the edict he had set down in the dining room. Elijah had never been the rule-abiding sort. Thel had once caught his brother with a set of shears in their mother's closet, slicing her favorite gown into pieces. When he'd asked why Elijah had done it, his brother had only shrugged and said, "I needed strips of cloth."

Thel slid his notebook back into his desk. "What has Olivia done to set you all against her?"

Elijah scowled. "You call her by her given name?"

Thel's cheeks heated. "Lady Allen is a respectable woman, no matter what the newspapers say." He picked up a cigar from the open box on his desk but did not light it. "In any case, I am Constance's father, and our father's heir. It is my duty to see to her future."

Elijah made no further comment, but the disharmony in the house was worrisome. The family should have supported his decision regarding Constance. They should have come together to ensure her debut was successful and free of scandal. Instead, they were bickering like children. If the fighting continued, it would not be long before his Felix sought his own accommodations. The family was a delicate ecosystem. Once Felix and his wife and children left, it would not be long before Elijah followed. Every member of his family would go their separate ways, and he would have no chance of convincing Constance and her future husband to live with him. He would be left alone and without purpose.

Again.

He could not let that happen. They had been happy before, and could be so again, even if it meant letting Felix have his way.

Lady Allen was his last chance. No other matchmaker had been willing to abide by his requirements. If she could not secure a love match for Constance, a suitor who met with his brother's approval, he would allow Felix to present him with options for an arranged marriage.

One way or another, his daughter would be married by the end of the season.

Chapter Seven

O LIVIA STOMPED ACROSS the gleaming marble, not sparing a second to admire the vivid paintings and perfectly polished statues along the walls of Lord Lowell's home.

Madame Julian had not been the last to refuse them. Oh, no. They had visited a dozen other modistes in an increasing fervor before finally ordering the carriage back.

The day could not have been more of a failure.

She clasped her hands at her waist to prevent herself from flapping them. She would not be foiled so easily. There had to be a way, someone she had overlooked.

Lord Lowell entered the room. "Lady Allen, I did not expect you back so soon."

The words flew from her lips. "They rejected me! Oh!" She gathered the shreds of her self-control and straightened her back. "We must speak in private, my lord."

"I agree." He held out his arm.

It was a gentlemanly offer, one she should have immediately accepted. The problem was that she didn't want to touch him. Her skin itched as if she had spent too long in the bath and the closer she came to the marquess, the more the feeling intensified. He was the cause of her problems. If it were not for him, she wouldn't have suffered such embarrassment.

"What is it?" he asked, frowning.

"Nothing of importance," she said. Then she forced a smile

and placed her fingers on his sleeve.

They strolled down the hall, past closed doors, and paintings with silver etched frames. The stern faces of Lord Lowell's ancestors, judging her from the past.

When the marquess and the dowager countess entered Lord Lowell's office, a silver-haired woman in a severe black dress stood from a chair and faced them.

"Constance's governess turned lady's maid, Mrs. Quill," Lord Lowell said. "Mrs. Quill, this is the matchmaker I mentioned, the Countess Dowager Allen."

The woman dipped into a deep curtsey. "A pleasure to meet you, Lady Allen."

Olivia murmured something appropriate before crossing the room to the collection of crystal bottles next to the wall. Her nerves were scattered, her face was hot, and her hands were sore from clenching them all morning. In sum, she was well in need of alcohol.

Lord Lowell met her at the sideboard and poured two fingers of bourbon into a glass from a crystal decanter. "What happened?"

She downed the liquid. It had a sickly-sweet taste like overripe cherries and clung to the inside of her mouth. "The articles happened. Every modiste in London has seen them."

"I see." He grimaced. "Then there is no choice. We must put a stop to the articles immediately."

She clenched her teeth to keep a snarl from bursting from her lips. "*Now* you're willing to negotiate? You might have saved me a day of embarrassment."

He paused in the middle of removing a cork from a bottle of wine. "P-Pardon?"

She folded her arms over her chest so that he would not see how they trembled. "Cease these games, my lord. I agreed to your ridiculous terms. There is no reason for you to continue your attacks. If you don't stop, I cannot promise that I will be able to find an appropriate match for your daughter. The rumors have already spread farther than I expected."

He poured himself a glass of red wine. "You're accusing me of contributing to those articles about you." Then he went silent, staring at his glass for so long that her temper began to rise again.

"Yes. Well?" she asked. "Do you intend to do something?"

He grimaced. "I was considering taking the blame, but I suspect it would not be long before you discovered the truth. Perhaps it is best that we decide what to do together." He removed a bundle of envelopes wrapped in a ribbon from his pocket and handed them to her. "I found these in Constance's room. Mrs. Quill has already reviewed them."

She stared at the bundle. "What's this?" Her role as matchmaker did not require her to read her charges' private correspondence. Doing so would be a violation of trust.

He sipped his wine. "They aren't what they look like."

She reluctantly untied the ribbon and unfolded the first of the envelopes. As she read, the room seemed to close around her.

"There must be some other explanation," Mrs. Quill said. She had resumed sitting but was perched at the edge of the chair. "I know Constance's handwriting and it doesn't match what's in the letters."

"She could have had someone else write them," Lord Lowell said.

Mrs. Quill shook her head. "No. She could never... I cannot believe she would use your name to do such evil, my lord. What reason would she have for attacking Lady Allen?"

Olivia felt as if she were floating out of her body. Mrs. Quill transformed into her mother, pacing in front of the fireplace while her father nursed his third glass of whiskey.

"This cannot be happening," her mother had said. "There must be some other explanation. What did he promise you, Olivia?"

"He's bedded her," her father had replied. "What other reason can there be?"

That statement had been wrong, but her denials had not

stopped her parents from punishing her as if she had ruined herself.

She licked her dry lips and opened the next envelope in the packet with numb fingers. There was no letter inside, but a collection of newspaper clippings, starting with the very first article that had attacked her. A dawning realization settled over her as she flipped through them.

The writing, the cadence, the cowardice. How had she not seen it before? It was as if her late husband were speaking the words in her mind.

Only a man was capable of such cruelty.

Lord Lowell put his wineglass down and squared his shoulders. "Lady Allen, I swear on my honor that I had no knowledge of my daughter's actions before today. You are within your rights to demand a retraction, but I request that my daughter's name be kept out of the papers."

Mrs. Quill huffed. "The girl must learn a lesson."

"Constance didn't write these," Olivia said.

The other two occupants of the room stared at her as if she had unsheathed a sword from behind her back.

"Why do you think that?" Lord Lowell asked.

"Has Constance been distracted lately? Showing less interest in activities she once enjoyed? Staying in her room more often?"

Mrs. Quill shifted in her seat. "She is at a difficult age."

It was the same pattern of behavior Olivia's parents had noticed and remarked upon during Olivia's tumultuous first season. What they had not known was that the Earl of Allen had inserted himself into her life long before he'd begun publicly courting her. He had preyed on her loneliness, undermining her shaky relationship with her parents, until he'd been the only person she trusted.

It wasn't until years later that she understood that alienating her, manipulating her, torturing her, were the things the earl had loved most. That was why he had caused such chaos in her life rather than simply present his suit to her parents properly.

He had not wanted a wife. He'd wanted a victim.

She took a deep breath. She might be wrong, but there were too many similarities to remain silent. "I believe the articles were written by a man who has cultivated a relationship with Constance as part of a scheme to exact revenge against me."

The silence was interrupted by a loud crash elsewhere in the house, followed by screeching laughter. Mrs. Quill leaped to her feet with a muttered curse and raced out, leaving them alone.

Olivia carefully tucked the sheets of paper into their respective envelopes and then held out the stack to Lord Lowell. "Put these back where you found them before she notices."

He frowned. "Why would I do that?"

She lowered her arm. "Think about it. First, the articles accuse me of murder. Then every matchmaker in London refuses you, leading you to me. Now we discover Constance is involved with those same articles. It cannot be a coincidence." She paused to swallow the saliva that had accumulated in her mouth. This next part was awkward, but it was necessary to make him understand. "I believe someone is using the same techniques the Earl of Allen used against me before our marriage to manipulate Constance into destroying my reputation."

It was a cruel manner of revenge, which suggested a personal motive. That meant she could rule out any mamas who might have been angry at her for rejecting their daughters. She could not imagine a mother being willing to sacrifice another young woman for something so petty. The new earl was also unlikely to be the culprit. He had only appeared in London briefly for the funeral and had expressed little interest in his new title.

"Why Constance?" Lord Lowell asked, his voice breaking. "Why my daughter?"

His dismay stabbed at her heart. She'd been so furious with him for feigning innocence when it hadn't been an act at all.

She dropped her gaze to the floor. "I'm sorry, my lord. Perhaps she was simply an easy target. The only thing I am certain of is that I am at fault. Someone wants to hurt me and is using

Constance to do it."

Olivia could not summon any anger toward the girl. They had too much in common, having both been ensnared by the worst kind of man. If anything, the blame for Constance's current situation fell on her father, for allowing her to stumble into a trap.

He sighed. "I am as much at fault as you. If I had been paying more attention, I would have noticed the change in her behavior. I was too focused on fulfilling the promise I made to her mother." He poured the rest of the wine bottle into his glass. "I will speak to Constance and put an end to the articles."

"No."

He paused in the process of picking up his glass. "You would have her continue?"

She remembered what her parents had done after they had discovered her connection to the earl. They had locked her in her room and deprived her of food. She'd told them what they'd wanted to hear, then ran back to the earl the first chance she'd gotten. Her relationship with them had never improved. They had gone to their graves before she'd had a chance to repair the damage the earl had done.

"If we interfere, we tip our hand. Whoever is manipulating Constance will know they've been discovered and might find another way of using her to get to me. I can't..." She swallowed the lump that had formed in her throat. A lifetime of pain whirled within her and demanded she act. "I won't let a girl under my care fall victim to a man like that." She held the envelopes out again. "Trust me. Constance doesn't know what she's doing. You must let her come to me on her own."

"I don't like this." He slammed his glass down on the sideboard and snatched the envelopes so quickly and with such a stormy expression that her instincts kicked in. She flung her hands in front of her face to blunt the blows that would come next.

But nothing happened.

Of course nothing happened. He was not her late husband. He didn't throw fists at a woman simply because she said something he disliked.

She tucked her arms behind her back and met his gaze. The confusion and hurt she saw there made her heart leap into her throat. He was so close that if she puffed out her chest, her bodice would brush his jacket, but she could not make herself move.

"What's wrong?" he asked.

The reassuring words she knew she should say remained trapped in her mind. She shook her head so quickly that the jet beads hanging from her hat smacked her on the cheek.

He brushed his knuckles against her chin. "What happened to you?"

A knock at the door had them flying apart, like lovers caught in a shadowy alcove at a ball. She had not felt so skittish since she was a young girl.

The door opened and Mrs. Quill peered in, her shoulders slumped. "The twins knocked over two of your great-grandmother's vases, my lord."

He straightened, all traces of the soft-spoken man who had caressed her cheek gone. "Are they well?"

Mrs. Quill winced. "The vases are beyond repair, I'm afraid."

Olivia tensed, remembering how she had once dropped a plate in front of her husband. He had sulked for days, showing her through his neglect that he disapproved of her clumsiness. She had never handled any dishes in front of him again without suffering significant anxiety.

"Damn the vases," he said. "Where are the twins? I'll see to them myself and ensure they know there are no bad feelings."

With those words, the last remaining threads of Olivia's suspicion slipped away. Lord Lowell did not have an ounce of cruelty in him. Regardless of what Constance had done, he was not her nemesis.

"Perhaps later," Mrs. Quill said. "A woman has arrived, my lord. She, ah, did not give her name, but she was quite insistent that she speak to you both at once regarding Lady Constance."

"Direct her to my daughter's room," he said. "We will see what she has to say."

Chapter Eight

A s Lady Allen placed her trembling fingers on Thel's sleeve, he wished he could draw her close and whisper soft words in her ear. He might have done so, except that he feared she might bolt. He'd never had a woman recoil from him before. Instead of thinking about how he was going to deal with his daughter's unknown paramour, he was preoccupied with how he might put Lady Allen's mind at ease.

The way she'd covered her face with her arms spoke of a history of violence. Someone, likely the deceased earl, had mistreated her. Anger smoldered in his gut as he imagined the innocent girl Lady Allen had once been. Cruelty had stripped that from her. It was no wonder she was so determined to help Constance. He wasn't sure he believed her claims that someone other than his daughter had written the letters, but he could not risk ignoring her. If a man had inserted himself into Constance's life, Thel wanted to know who it was.

They walked to Constance's room behind Mrs. Quill, then stepped inside as he opened the door. Constance sat before her dressing mirror, running a brush through her hair. The faraway look in her eyes suggested she hadn't even noticed them entering.

His heart gave a painful lurch as he imagined her gathering her pin money to send to the newspaper. The articles had started weeks ago, before they had ever come to London. How had he overlooked that she'd been hiding something so important? She had never kept secrets from him.

Lady Allen had told him to place the envelopes back where he had found them, but as a father, he wanted to throw them onto Constance's desk and demand answers.

He was slipping his hand in his pocket when Lady Allen grabbed his sleeve and whispered, "While she is distracted."

He retrieved the envelopes but held firm when she tried to tug them out of his grasp. It felt wrong to be sneakily returning items he had taken from Constance's room. She might have hidden things from him, but he did not want to do the same. Admitting what he had done might cause a rift to form between them, but it would show her he valued honesty.

He cleared his throat.

Constance caught his gaze in the mirror and shot upright. The brush fell out of her hand and clattered onto the floor. "Yes, Father?"

He held out the ribbon-wrapped bundle. "I found these in your room."

"What are you—" Olivia started, but he spoke over her.

"I removed these because I was concerned that... you..." His impromptu lecture faded as Constance tilted her head and frowned.

He waggled the envelopes. "Have you seen these before?"

She shook her head. "You found those in my room? What are they?" She stepped forward and reached for the bundle, but he moved his hand out of reach.

She did not know what he was talking about.

The room spun as he was overcome with relief. He'd been wrong. Constance had had nothing to do with the articles. Except that didn't quite fit. If they weren't Constance's doing, then who had hidden the letters he had found in her room? It had to be someone in his household, as they had not been in London long enough for Constance to have callers.

"Let me see," his daughter said. She went up on her toes and grabbed for the envelopes. When she was unable to reach, she stomped her foot and pouted. "Why are you hiding things from me?"

Before he could come up with an excuse, a short woman with fiery-red hair shoved past them into the room, hefting bolts of pink-and-white fabric on her shoulders.

"Where is the lass?" she asked.

He stepped into the woman's path. "Who are you?"

"Lily, how wonderful!" Lady Allen said, stepping around him. "It has been an age. Did Lady Briarwood send you?"

"Aye, my lady." She dropped the bolts of fabric ends down on the carpet with a loud *thud*. "I've come to outfit the lass for the season."

"Thank God," Lady Allen said. "You are our savior."

Then Lily turned to the door and shouted, "Lads, bring them here!"

He staggered back as a line of servants filed in, carrying trunks or armfuls of fabric in colors ranging from pale yellow to rich cobalt while Constance flitted around them, barely muffling her squeals of excitement.

Lady Allen clung to his side. He curled his arm around her waist before catching himself. His excitement at Constance's reaction to the envelopes had left him giddy.

"She didn't recognize them," he said. "What does that mean?"

Lady Allen pursed her lips. "Are you sure she isn't lying?"

He throttled down the immediate urge to fly to his daughter's defense. As much as he thought he knew her, he was too sensible to believe it was a coincidence that the letters they found were addressed to the same newspaper that was publishing articles attacking Olivia. It was much more likely that Constance, who was barely eighteen and on the cusp of making the most important decision of her life, had become skilled at lying to her father.

He sighed. "No. I'm not sure."

Lady Allen squeezed his bicep. "Have patience. I'll get the answer out of her in time."

He hoped she was right. Knowing that his daughter was hiding something from him was like walking around with a sliver embedded in his flesh. He longed to rid himself of the pain, but it was too deep to remove on his own.

It seemed like only yesterday Constance had shrieked with joy as he'd carried her on his shoulders around the house. Now she was entering society and preparing to choose a husband. The weekly allowance he gave her was a pittance compared to her dowry.

His thoughts screeched to a halt.

There was no way of proving if she was lying about the envelopes, but he could check the account he had opened for her. If she had paid the editor to publish the articles, there would certainly be large withdrawals.

He made his excuses to Lady Allen and his daughter and left them to sort out the dresses themselves.

He had an appointment with his banker.

Chapter Nine

THE MOMENT LORD Lowell left the room, the tension in Olivia's shoulders eased.

God, what he must think of her. One moment she was accusing him of slander and cringing from his touch, the next she was patting his arm and assuring him all would be well. She felt like a young woman again, at the mercy of the powerful emotions swirling inside her.

Then there was the matter of Constance and her involvement with the newspaper. She wished it was as simple as demanding the girl stop, but until they knew if Olivia was right about the girl being manipulated, it was too risky. If someone intended to ruin Olivia's reputation, confronting Constance might prompt them to escalate. Likewise, forcing Constance into a corner could tie her more firmly to the man who was manipulating her. Not that she had any proof that it wasn't Constance herself who had arranged the articles. It was Olivia's instincts that warned her the situation was not as simple as it seemed.

No, the best course of action was to earn the girl's trust by continuing in her role as matchmaker. Even if it meant confronting memories she had repressed since the earl's death.

She lifted a length of lavender satin that slid along her skin like a caress and carried it to Constance. "How do you feel about this for an evening gown?"

Constance ran her hand along the fabric. "It's beautiful. I

cannot wait to attend my first event." Her eyes glazed over. "Sometimes I imagine I'm a princess invited to a royal ball, dancing with princes from each country until I find one who..." She flushed. "My apologies, Lady Allen. Mrs. Quill says I am prone to flights of fancy."

An ache started in Olivia's chest. Constance reminded her so much of herself, before her imagination had been routed out, first by her parents, then by her governess, and finally by her husband.

She would not be like them. Constance deserved to enjoy every moment of her adolescence before she was thrust into the role of wife and then mother.

Olivia picked up the bolt of satin, draped it around her shoulders, and swished it around like a cape. "You might be a princess, but I am a queen, watching over the grand ball from my throne upon the dais."

Constance's mouth fell open, but it did not take her long to recover.

"There's something missing." She raced over to her dressing table and plucked a silver tiara from atop her jewelry box.

Olivia knelt as the girl returned and placed the sparkling piece atop her head. When she straightened, she pitched her voice high and said, "Good evening, Lady Constance. Have you been introduced to my son?" She scooped up one of Constance's hats and placed it atop a bolt of black linen. "He is quite shy, I'm afraid."

Constance wrapped herself in a shimmering pink chiffon. "Good evening, Your Highness. Pardon? Oh, yes, I would be honored to share your first dance."

Constance grabbed the bolt and bounced around the trunks, while Olivia hummed a lively polka tune. She could almost imagine they were at St. James's Palace, a venue she had only visited once, the year she had come out. She would never forget the anxiety of kneeling before the queen in her best dress, and the unfathomable relief of earning no more or less than a nod from the monarch.

"What is going on here?" Lily asked.

Olivia froze as reality crashed down on her. Yards of fabric pooled at her feet, spilling across the floor and over several trunks. She had gone far beyond encouraging Constance and allowed her fantasies to take hold.

"I apologize," she said, snatching the tiara from her head.

Lily's frown eased. "'Tis no worry, my lady. I'll have it cleaned up in a trice."

Olivia didn't want it cleaned up. She wanted to dance in the spilled fabric, to lose herself in her imagination and forget, for a few minutes, everything that had happened in the past week. Or, more accurately, the past decade.

"Of course," Olivia said. "I apologize again for our exuberance."

Lily clucked her tongue and positioned Constance onto a circular dressing stand as her helpers wheeled into the room. The maid wasted no time in wrapping her charge in strips of paper, jotting down each measurement in a small notebook.

It was tiresome to watch, and even more to sit through, so she was not surprised when Constance began to fidget. Olivia knew she should keep her silence to avoid embarrassing herself further, but she also had a job to do. Regardless of Constance's involvement in the articles, she would not allow any girl in her care to wade into a season without preparation. There were too many men ready and willing to swoop in and play "the hero" to soiled doves, with no thought of marriage.

She met Constance's gaze in the mirror and asked, "Have you ever seen your father speak cruelly to a servant?"

Constance looked appalled. "Never."

"Have you ever seen him shout at a woman, servant or otherwise? Has he ever whipped a horse into a lather and then refused to take care of the beast when it was done with its work?"

Constance shook her head. "He would never do such things."

"But if you had only seen him at balls, or garden parties, how would you know he is not a cruel man?"

This was a question she wished someone had brought up when she'd been a debutante. She hadn't understood then how the aspect one showed in society was a falsehood. That was likely the reason she'd made no friends in her year, and how the earl had insinuated himself into her life so readily.

Constance screwed up her lips. "I don't know."

"Precisely. But there are ways you can ensure that a suitor is not cruel."

"How?"

"For one, compliments that are not complimentary. I once heard Mr. Rutlidge tell Miss Whisperwill that her lovely, orange gown was the same shade as his favorite cat's fur. Miss Whisperwill, an animal lover, was quite pleased with this comparison, until Mr. Rutlidge asked if he should check beneath her skirts for a tail."

Constance hissed, surprising Olivia into a laugh. The next moment, she was hissing right back and holding her hands as if she had claws. Lily, from beneath Constance's dress, uttered a series of words that Olivia didn't recognize, and then scurried out from beneath the hulking fabric.

"Enough with both of you," Lily said, sticking her thumb in her mouth. "I'll bleed myself to death before this is up."

Olivia gulped. "My apologies."

Constance was in fits, but Lily was scowling, which did not bode well for Olivia or her relationship with Lily's employer.

So as much as it pained her, she sat demurely on the couch and only called a halt to the dress fittings when Constance had to be reminded to straighten her back three times in as many minutes by a snappish Lily.

The room was uncomfortably warm, even as the fluttering curtain drew in a breeze that carried the smell of freshly cut grass. If she were at her townhouse, with its private backyard, she might have run through the lawn with her bare feet, but she did not have the luxury at the marquess's home. Instead, she said farewell to Constance and left Lily and her helpers to clean up the mess they had made of the room. Constance would have gowns, at least. Lily had already pinned together the pieces of several dresses that were going to be lovely when they were finished.

She made a mental note to send Saffron a letter of thanks, as they would occupy Lily for some time.

"Lady Allen?"

She stopped. In her musing, she hadn't realized that she had walked to Lord Lowell's office. He stood in the doorway, a newspaper tucked beneath his arm. His cravat was missing, and his shirt was half-unbuttoned, revealing a tantalizing amount of muscular chest.

"Is everything all right?" he asked.

"Y-Yes, of course." She wrenched her gaze back to his face. "The dress fittings went well."

"I am glad to hear it." He stepped closer. "I've just come from the bank. I checked Constance's account, and it was nearly depleted."

The news was not a surprise but made her feel as if she had swallowed a stone. It was difficult to believe the girl she'd danced with had paid to have such awful things published.

"There is something else," he said. "I sent a footman to the office of the *London Evening Standard* and got a copy of tomorrow's edition. Perhaps you should see it before you return home."

She steeled herself for the worst and accepted the newspaper. It was folded to display the newest article from her nemesis. As she read it, her face grew hot, and she had to tamper back the urge to tear the paper into shreds.

ACCUSED MURDERESS FAILS AGAIN. I am pleased to inform the esteemed readers of the London Evening Standard *that Lady Allen has failed in her latest attempt to prevent the spread of truth. There is no alternative now than to reveal the full extent of her crimes. It did not start on the night of the earl's death, but a fortnight earlier, when the cowardly woman began dosing her husband's nightly draught with laudanum.*

MENTOR TO THE MARQUESS

With the earl unconscious, the seductress donned a cloak and crept out of her marital home to pursue her wicked endeavors. However, the men who imbibed of her flesh should not be blamed. They are as much victims of feminine wiles as the cuckolded earl, who, after many nights of restless sleep, caught wind of her schemes. On his final night, he refused to drink her potion, and in doing so received his ultimate gift—a fatal dose forced down his throat.

How did her enemy know she had dosed the earl? They had refused visitors the days before he'd passed, and she had told no one, not even Saffron, of the earl's pain. Laudanum had been the only thing that had brought him peace. Only the two of them and a handful of staff knew.

Staff.

That was the answer. Her enemy must have paid one of her former maids. If so, they were likely in possession of far more damning information. She was not proud of all that had happened during the earl's final hours, when he had become delirious with fever.

"Is it true?" he asked softly.

"There is an element of truth," she said, without looking at him. She didn't want him to see how upset she felt, or it would open the floodgates and she wouldn't be able to stop feeling.

That had been the case in the early days of her marriage. The earl would say something to set her off, some cruel insult or barbed comment, and it would cause her to lie in bed and sob for hours, lost to misery. It had taken her until the age of thirty to learn that if she was neutral, unfeeling, she could not be hurt.

The marquess put his hands on her shoulders, a shockingly intimate gesture, as his thumbs grazed the tops of her breasts.

"You don't need to pretend with me," he said.

She knew she should reciprocate, encourage him with a flutter of her long lashes or a gentle sigh. That was what Lady Allen would do now that there was no longer any reason to resist her attraction. But Lady Allen felt a million miles away, and it was

Olivia trapped beneath his touch.

Her jaw trembled, and a tear slipped down her cheek. She quickly brushed it away and put some distance between them. "It is nothing," she said, relieved when her voice held no trace of tremor.

He tugged her into his office, then closed the door and locked it.

Her mouth went dry. "My lord, what are—"

He wrapped his arms around her. One hand cupped the back of her head, the other curled around her waist, trapping her against him. She didn't have the willpower to push him away, not when the solid muscle beneath her fingertips made her want to melt into his embrace.

The impropriety of the moment made her freeze, yet he didn't kiss her or make any overtures she recognized as the precursor to an intimate encounter. He only held her tightly, silently. She smelled soap on his skin, combined with the musk of his sweat, and relaxed.

The earl had never held her. Nor had most of her previous lovers. With rare exception, they had taken what they wanted, then left. She never let anyone stay beyond their coupling. There was no point. When both parties had achieved release, why extend the moment?

He released her and stepped back with jerky movements. "I apologize. I should not have done that."

The set of his shoulders. The pain in his voice. The tightening of his features. It was like seeing a reflection of herself from the early years of her marriage when the earl had punished her for failing to become pregnant by refusing to acknowledge her presence.

That simply would not do.

She closed the distance between them, went up on her toes, and brought their mouths together.

Chapter Ten

L ORD LOWELL'S LIPS were still against hers for the first few seconds before he wrapped his arms around her and pulled her tight. She slid her arms up his back, as far as she could reach. The rasp of his mustache and beard against her cheek made her skin erupt into gooseflesh.

She swept her tongue into his mouth, and a sound rumbled from his chest. He tasted of sweet wine and the hard ridge of his arousal dug into her stomach.

By the time he pulled away, her neck and shins were aching from lifting herself to his height.

He wiped his lips with the back of a hand, then grinned. "I have wanted to kiss you from the moment I set eyes on you, Lady Allen."

A nervous laugh bubbled up in her throat. "'Olivia,' please. I believe we are past formalities."

He slid hands down her arms and tangled their fingers together. "Only if you use my given name as well."

She licked her lips. "Thellusson?"

He snorted. "Only my mother calls me that. It's 'Thel.'"

"Thel," she whispered.

It felt so intimate. A name she could whisper in the dark.

He tugged her to a couch and sat down, pulling her to sit beside him. He cleared his throat. "How... was it?"

Of all the things she had expected him to say, that was not

one of them.

"It was lovely, but..." She wasn't sure how to express her thoughts. She recognized the uncertainty in his tone, the skittishness she had dealt with countless times in the girls she sponsored. But what her instincts were telling her was impossible. He had been married. He had a child. This was no virgin, but a man nearly ten years her senior.

"When was the last time you were with a woman?" she blurted out.

He sighed. "Not since my wife passed. There are... reasons. I am not, ah, incapable, I assure you."

She placed a hand on his thigh. "I do not doubt that." His trousers were clearly tented. Whatever his reason, it was not a physical one. At the same time, she had been a mistress for enough married men who claimed to be satisfied with their wives that she had to ask the obvious question. "You never considered taking a paramour?"

He ran a hand through his hair. "I did. Many nights. But every time I thought I was ready, I imagined what Marguerite would say." His throat worked. "I loved her so much. When she died, it almost killed me. Compared to what we had, a quick tup—even with an experienced lady—felt hollow. Meaningless. I couldn't do it." He shrugged. "I'm afraid I am woefully inexperienced."

The scenario he described was a stark contrast to the coldness of her own marriage. She could not imagine being so attached to a person such that parting from them would cause her such grief. She'd hardly mourned the deaths of her own parents. But that did not mean she was not empathetic to his situation. Her heart ached for the pain he must have felt.

She drew in a breath. What she was about to suggest was scandalous. Dangerous, even. She'd carefully cultivated a mystique of an experienced woman, a lady whom a gentleman could take to his bed without fear of being blackmailed later. She'd managed this without earning scorn from society by carefully selecting her sexual partners. If even one of them spurned her, they could have her branded a loose woman. But despite barely knowing Thel, she felt she could trust him enough to give him what he so obviously needed.

"I could reacquaint you," she said. "I am an expert in several... unusual techniques."

"You would do that?" He frowned. "Your reputation..."

She laughed. "My lord, I am a widow. Becoming involved with you, a widower, is one of the least scandalous things I've ever done. If we are discreet, no one will care."

"In that case"—he slid his hand up her back—"I would be pleased to have you as my mentor."

She arched her back into his touch.

He added a second hand. "You like this. What else do you like?"

His eagerness would be the death of her.

"I believe we are wearing too many clothes," she said.

He yanked the edge of his shirt out of his trousers and lifted it over his head. She put a hand on his chest to stop him.

"First lesson," she said. "Undressing can be a sensual art. There is no need to hurry."

He flicked the buttons of his shirt open. As each came loose, more of his chest was revealed, carpeted with thick, black hair. When he finished, he ran his fingers down her sides. "Should you take this off as well?"

She nearly choked but recovered herself. "No, it would take too much time."

She cursed her choice of attire. Had she known what the day would bring, she would have donned a much more comfortable garment. One that was easier to remove.

He put his hand on his bare chest, then looked at hers. "This feels rather unfair."

The temptation to begin furiously shucking her clothing was strong, but she didn't feel comfortable enough in his home to reassemble herself.

That didn't mean she couldn't have fun.

She dipped her head and kissed his jaw and neck down to his chest and rasped a nipple with her tongue.

He cupped the back of her head with a hand and squeezed.

She lifted her head and pressed their mouths together. This time, he swept his tongue between her lips. His technique was sloppy, but the eagerness with which he kissed her combined with the feel of his hands massaging her hips made dampness flow to her sex.

That was for another time, however. She did not want to rush ahead when they had so much territory to explore. When she felt him throbbing beneath her, she withdrew.

"That was…" He uttered a short laugh. "You have rendered me speechless." He caressed her cheek with the back of his fingers. "Would it be impertinent to ask what you are thinking?"

She laughed. "You do not want to know what I am thinking, my lord."

If she told him, they might not leave his office until morning.

"Is it not expected for a mentor to assess her student's performance?"

She laughed again, harder this time. "You want me to critique your technique?"

Her past partners had only ever cared about her pleasure in its capacity to increase their own. If she had dared offer suggestions to the earl, he would have given her the back of his hand.

"How else will I improve?" Thel asked.

The sincerity in his voice left her speechless. Who was this man who believed in love and was so devoted to his partner that he was willing to risk his ego being bruised?

"I'll consider your request," she said. Then she rose from his lap and righted her clothes. Only when she reached the door did she feel able to speak.

"Until tomorrow."

"Until our next lesson," he replied.

OLIVIA ROLLED ONTO her stomach the next morning and buried her face in her pillow. It smelled faintly of coal from the metal heater tucked beneath her mattress. Without it, the bed would have been ice cold. Of course, if she'd stayed with Thel, she wouldn't have needed the contraption. The man radiated more warmth than the smoldering embers of a fire. He was earnest, kind, and gentle. The exact opposite of her former husband.

Her mind was drawn back to the moment in Thel's office when he'd held her. It was unusual to find such an intimidating man who was so gentle. It made her want to protect him, to preserve his innocence despite the fierce desire of the *ton* to root out such things like stubborn weeds. Thel's sensitive soul needed to be carefully cultivated, not shorn down to make way for more socially acceptable traits.

London had enough brutish managing men. They did not need another.

A gentle rap came at the door.

"Enter," she said.

Her butler stepped inside. His dour face was even more pinched than usual, his thin eyebrows drawn together. "Pardon the interruption, my lady, but Lady Briarwood has arrived."

That was exactly what she needed. Someone with whom to commiserate.

"Show her in," Olivia said.

The door closed, and moments later, flew open again. Saffron clutched a rolled-up newspaper in her hand, which she slammed on the table.

"I've seen it," Olivia said.

Any whispers she might have received at events would increase tenfold now that there were specific details for the *ton* to chew over.

"I had Leo reach out to the editor, but the man would not

budge," Saffron said, falling back onto the horsehair sofa. "What happened with Lord Lowell? I thought you had made a deal."

Olivia winced. "It would not matter if I did. He's not the source behind the articles."

Saffron patted the seat beside her. "Tell me everything."

Olivia perched on the edge of the couch and carefully described the events of the previous day. Saffron's mouth fell open at one point, but she remained blessedly silent until Olivia finished.

"You have certainly been busy," Saffron said, swirling a spoon around her teacup.

Olivia sipped her lukewarm tea. It tasted bitter and there was soapy residue on the porcelain. She set the cup down with a grimace. In her obsession to discover who'd been slandering her name, she'd neglected her own household. The gaslights were covered in cobwebs, the furnace was thick with soot and ashes, and now even the tableware was not up to snuff.

She sank into the pillows on the couch. "How do I lure my enemy out?"

She didn't know his name or title. She didn't even know if there was a man at all, only that her instincts insisted Constance could not have written the letters on her own. So many assumptions, and little to no facts. It was no way to run an investigation.

"Have you considered staging a counterattack?" Saffron asked.

Olivia tucked a pillow behind her back. "What do you mean?"

"The newspapers with the latest article have already been printed and distributed. It is too late to prevent that. But what if you were to attack using the same means?"

"You mean write a response?" Olivia sniffed. "I doubt the editor would print it. He made it abundantly clear how much he values my opinion."

"Because you approached him as yourself."

Olivia straightened. "Are you proposing...?"

"Yes!" Saffron bounced in her seat. "Take the name of a man

and make a rebuttal. I can transcribe for you. Summon a maid to bring us the supplies. I have always wanted to play secretary."

Olivia was quickly swept up in Saffron's excitement. The maid who brought her traveling writing desk did not ask why she needed it, but the confused expression on the young girl's face assured Olivia that her servants would discuss this visit for days to come.

Saffron set the mahogany box on her lap and withdrew a pen and a sheet of parchment. "How should we begin?"

Olivia picked up the glass of brandy she had poured while waiting for the maid. "We follow the cadence of his articles. That way, no one can miss the intent." She sipped her drink, savored the fruity sweetness and the slight burn down her throat, then set her glass down and began dictating.

Chapter Eleven

SLANDEROUS RUMORS. Accusations have recently been made about Lady Allen, which have not been substantiated with evidence. A counterargument could therefore be raised that said accuser is a former paramour of said lady, who cannot see her in the arms of another. Why else would he be obsessed with her past? One only need look in a mirror to understand that those who protest too much are confessing the sins they proclaim of others.

THERE WERE ONLY so many hours in a day one could read before even that became tiresome.

Olivia slouched into the plush upholstery of a velvet sofa in Thel's drawing room. The gloomy morning light streamed in through the narrow windows and made the air sparkle with dust. She flipped a page, continuing the story of a romance of peculiar interest involving a murderous barber and an innovative, if disturbed, baker. It was one of her favorite penny dreadfuls, as exciting as it was gruesome, but she could not seem to engage properly.

She had occupied the previous afternoon and evening searching through her correspondence for clues about who might have a reason to want to ruin her reputation. Then she'd spent a restless night alone, remembering how good it had felt to be in Thel's arms.

It is mere infatuation, nothing more.

Certainly not a reason to be concerned. It had been with Constance in mind that she had arrived at Thel's home so early that morning, prepared for the awkwardness of facing the girl's father, only to find he was out on some errand. That wouldn't have been an issue, except she had received no invitations to events for the day.

During the height of the season. When every venue in the city had been fully booked for months.

She could not decide if it was the articles that had caused society to shun her, or an angry Mrs. Zephyr fanning the flames of gossip as revenge for Olivia agreeing to be a matchmaker for Constance.

Probably both.

But she would not give up so easily. It would take time to earn Constance's trust enough for the girl to confide in her, and continuing in her role as matchmaker would allow her to establish herself in Constance's life.

Constance, who had shown no signs of resentment toward her matchmaker despite the ferocity of the attacks that she'd been manipulated to participate in. The girl lounged on a divan with a book, her stockinged feet hanging over the edge in a posture that would have driven a governess to distraction, a lock of hair in her mouth.

It wasn't that Olivia hadn't been fooled before—she'd willingly married a monster—but she found it difficult to believe that Constance could secretly hate her. Olivia had not spent much time with the girl, but she seemed the kind to wear her emotions openly, even when it earned her reprimands from adults.

A booming sound somewhere in the house made her drop her book on her chest. Not that it mattered. She had read the same page three times.

Constance rose from her seat on the other side of the room. "Callers?"

The doors burst open, and several figures hurried inside.

"Grandmother!" Constance cried. She leaped from her seat

and ran toward an older, blonde woman in a mustard-yellow muslin gown. A man in a gray suit with a matching yellow shirt stood behind her, his expression speaking of fondness. He opened his arms and Constance flew into them.

Strange, sharp sensations swirled in Olivia's chest. Neither of her parents had ever invited her embrace. They had remained abstract concepts throughout her childhood. Her governess had raised her in their place, hammering the rules of society into her one lesson at a time.

Don't slouch. Don't rock back and forth. Don't stare into the distance when someone is talking to you.

What if Thel's parents disagreed with their son and wanted to find a husband for Constance themselves? She would have a hard time countering their wishes.

She clutched her hands tightly at her waist, relieved she had chosen a demure outfit for the day. The deep-purple morning gown had a high neckline, long sleeves, and jet buttons down the front. The cuffs had small tufts of lilac knotted lace, and the bodice came to a V in the front. It was one of her favorites for its comfort—it was lined with the softest silk faille—and because it allowed her to blend into a crowd rather than stand out.

At last, Thel's mother met her gaze. "You must be Lady Allen."

Olivia dropped into a deep curtsey. "I am pleased to meet you, Your Grace."

The Duke of Hestia squinted at her. "Who is this, then?"

The duchess tutted. "Dear, this is the woman who will find our darling Connie a husband." She turned her bright smile on Olivia. "It is a beautiful day. Why aren't you out enjoying the company of potential suitors?"

Now was the difficult part: telling them that her reputation was the reason for their lack of options, while avoiding any mention of their granddaughter's involvement.

Constance beat her to it.

"We have nowhere to go," the girl said.

The duchess's fine eyebrows flew up. "Nonsense. No one would ever deny us entrance."

"Do not tempt her," Thel said, entering the room.

The sound of his voice sent Olivia's heart thundering and when his gaze met hers, shivers went down her spine. He was even more handsome than he had been the previous day in a beige suit atop a checkered navy shirt. The color accentuated the fine, silver hairs at his temple and in his beard and drew her attention to the width of his shoulders.

"Oh, Thel," the duchess said. "As always, you spoil our fun."

Olivia looked back and forth between mother and son, not quite understanding what was happening. Were they suggesting they show up at an event without an invitation? It would be the height of rudeness.

Then again…

Lately, she had felt like a circus animal, forced to go against her nature and perform elaborate acts for the enjoyment of society. If they were going to call her scandalous, perhaps she would be truly scandalous.

"Let's do it," she said.

Constance squealed.

The duchess clapped her hands. "Wonderful!"

Thel shook his head. "I appear to have been outvoted." Then he walked to Olivia's side and offered his arm. "Shall we discuss our options?"

She nodded and allowed him to lead her back to his office. Except this time, when he led her into the room, he paused and glanced behind him. "I should have a servant inform Mrs. Quill that Constance will require her. Wait here a moment."

When he left, she wandered over to his desk and picked up a leatherbound book. She flipped it open to the first page and immediately recognized it for what it was. How many times had she lain awake, re-imagining the endings of her favorite books? In this handwritten story, which took place in the world of *Lady Audley's Secret*, the main character, George, shared a tender moment with his wife, who was still alive.

She had almost finished the first chapter when the book was snatched out of her hands by a red-faced Thel.

"I'm sorry," she said. "I didn't realize it was private."

Thel worried his bottom lip between his teeth. "What did you think?"

It was suddenly, painfully, obvious he was the writer. Another remarkable trait she hadn't expected him to possess. The man surprised her at every turn.

"I loved it," she said quickly. No other answer would suffice. She did not want to crush his spirit.

He grinned. "Truly? I worried I made the main characters too unlike how they are in the book."

"It's an improvement," she said. "In the book, the character of George is abrasive, almost unlikeable. Your version of him is much more appealing." He flipped through the pages, then held the book out. "There is another section I think you would enjoy."

She dropped her gaze and read. It was another scene with the same characters. Her eyes flew over the lines until she reached a bit that made her jaw drop. In the scene, George caught Helen snooping through his desk and metered out a rather titillating form of punishment.

"Do you like it?"

She set the book on his desk, then spun around and put her palms on his chest. "After reading that, I wonder if *you* should be the teacher, and I the student."

He wrapped his arms around her waist. "My knowledge was gained through research, not experience."

"Perhaps we should bridge the two."

She had always wondered what it might be like to take on a role as part of amorous congress. It was something the earl would have been eager to try, except the role he would've made her take would've been far from pleasant. But the earl was no longer around to constrain her.

She leaned over the marquess's desk and assumed an exaggerated posture of shock, with one hand at her breast and the other on her cheek. "H-Husband, you are home early! I promise I was only looking for a letter opener."

Thel ruffled his hair, tilted his head, and narrowed his eyes. "This is the third time I've caught you rifling around my desk this week, wife, after I told you to stay out of this room. You must be disciplined." He gestured toward the desk. "Assume the position."

The command in his tone had her hands trembling as she leaned over, jutting her rear out as far as she could. It was an awkward pose to hold, but she did not intend to be in it long.

Thel flipped her voluminous skirts up and over her head, obscuring her sight and leaving her nearly bare to him, from the waist to the ankle, aside from her drawers and stockings.

The first shock of his palm on the tender flesh of her rear made her knees wobble. She squeezed her thighs together, but it did not stop the pulse of sensation. She tolerated three of the same before she had enough.

"Please, husband, I cannot bear any more of this treatment," she said.

He scooped her up and set her on top of a cabinet. It was rickety and hard on her rear, but she could meet his gaze without craning her neck.

"Is it too soon to ask for another lesson?" he asked.

She licked her lips. "I was hoping you would ask."

He slid his hand beneath her skirt. "I would like to see what I am doing. May I undress you?"

"Yes," she whispered, even though she ached for him to shove his fingers inside her. She was glad she had chosen undergarments that were easy to remove in anticipation of such an event.

He slipped her boots off, letting them thud to the floor. Then he hiked her drawers up to her knees and untied her garters and unrolled her stockings, one at a time.

He kissed the inside of her thigh at the spot where her drawers split, trailing kisses until he reached her quivering, sensitive mound, then passed over it, brushing the flesh with his beard, before kissing her other thigh to her feet. As his whiskers brushed her big toe, a jolt of pure lust shot up her leg and made her moan.

"Show me how to bring you pleasure," he said.

She guided him to the place that cried out for his touch.

"You are very wet here," he said as he slid his fingers along her crease. "You would accept my cock easily."

The rasp in his voice sent shivers up her back. She pressed his forefinger directly against her clitoris. "A circular motion works best." She moved his fingers accordingly, and a jolt of pleasure streaked down her legs. "If that does not work, then a back-and-forth motion." She demonstrated again and this time, the sensation was so sharp, it startled a whimper from her lips.

Thel chuckled. "Quite a powerful reaction."

His hand twitched, but she held him still as she clawed herself back from the edge of release. It had been months since she had been with a man who had truly satisfied her, much less a man of such a large stature. She distantly wondered if the rest of him was as impressive.

"What now?" he asked.

"Use your mouth and tongue in the same way you used your fingers," she replied. Merely speaking the words, voicing her demands, made her squirm.

He returned to her sex, peeling her apart layer by layer, before spearing inside her with his tongue in a sudden movement that had her back arching.

She squirmed, wanting more pressure, and he obligingly pressed harder. She was close, but it still wasn't enough.

There was, however, one thing that always worked.

She reached beneath the many layers of fabric. Without her having to ask, he gave her space, smoothing his palm along her thigh with one hand and freeing his cock with the other.

Knowing he was aroused by watching her pleasure herself was enough to push her over the edge. She clenched her muscles tight and spiraled into completion.

Chapter Twelve

THE LIGHTS HANGING from the boughs of the trees lining the path twinkled like stars, but as far as Olivia was concerned, they were nothing but dim flashes in the dark, and the vibrant flowers blooming around her were dull and lifeless.

She had selected the event from among the pile of invitations on Thel's desk with the assurances that the Duke of Haversham was a friend of his family. It seemed fitting, given that Mrs. Zephyr had only stepped aside when Thel had mentioned the duke's name. But despite Thel's nonchalance, her stomach twisted as they approached the entrance to the sprawling grounds behind Thel's parents and daughter.

Constance glanced over her shoulder, looking every inch her rank in a sapphire evening gown with a heart-shaped neckline and her hair braided and wrapped around her head like a crown. It was only when she tucked a golden curl between her lips that Olivia realized something might have been wrong. Then the duchess leaned toward her granddaughter, and they shared a whispered conversation. Constance met Olivia's gaze, and her cheeks pinkened. She directed a nasty scowl at Olivia, plucked the lock of hair from her mouth, and turned around, her head tilted higher.

"Did you see that?" Olivia asked Thel. The expression on Constance's face had held such malice. What had the duchess said to elicit such a reaction?

Thel looked around. "See what?"

"Your mother said something to Constance that made her look at me like…" She wasn't sure how to describe how the brief exchange had unsettled her.

Then they were next in line to be introduced, and Olivia's anxiety washed all other concerns away.

Her name was not on the guest list. She had seen ladies arrive at the doors of grand events, only to be turned away in disgrace. Such a cut might damage her reputation beyond saving.

She froze as they reached a wooden arch covered in pink and white roses. Her fingers clenched around Thel's arm. She tried to summon the cool confidence that was the hallmark of Lady Allen, but her feet refused to budge.

"Wait here," Thel whispered. He pried her fingers from his sleeve and walked over to a small podium she had not noticed in the shadows, where a footman was standing. The two men shared a quiet conversation before Thel returned.

"What did you do?" she asked.

"Smoothed the way," he said. Then he tugged her forward.

She reluctantly followed him, even as prickling started in her fingers and crept up her arms. She did not know which outcome would be worse: if she entered without her name being announced, or if she was turned away before anyone noticed she had arrived.

She was so focused on keeping her expression carefully neutral that she tripped over her own feet. Thel caught her before she could stumble forward. She was about to thank him when a footman standing near the door spoke over her.

"The Duke and Duchess of Hestia, the Marquess of Lowell, the Lady Constance Vaith, and the Countess Dowager Allen."

The tight coil in her stomach released. Whatever Thel had done had worked. None of the other guests had any reason to doubt she had been invited.

A handful of curious guests lingering near the arch glanced her way. She tensed, expecting whispers and snide comments, but she heard no snickering or snap of fans opening. The few ladies who met her gaze only widened their eyes and stepped aside. After the third time this happened, she leaned closer to Thel and whispered, "When was the last time your parents attended social events?"

He shrugged. "My mother prefers to spend her days in the country."

That explained it. The presence of the duke and duchess after such a long absence was enough to draw attention away from her. While she remained with them, she was sheltered from scandal. The lack of muttering made her feel as if she had been transported back in time to before the articles had begun. It should have brought relief, but there was a gnawing hollowness in her stomach.

If it were not for her, their granddaughter might never have been targeted. It was her fault there was conflict in their family, and she was taking advantage of their goodwill by riding along on their coattails.

They traversed the garden without incident and arrived at a grand marble staircase that led into the house. The duke and duchess proceeded up the steps toward the muted sound of an orchestra, but as Olivia made to follow them, Constance tugged her arm. The girl's face was pale, and her eyes were so wide, the whites were visible all around her irises. The vulnerable expression on her face was so different from the scowl the girl had given her in the receiving line that Olivia was rendered speechless. Which was the act: the innocent girl Olivia was seeing now, or the girl she'd glimpsed earlier?

"What do I do if someone asks me to dance?" Constance whispered. "This is my first ball."

Olivia set her suspicions aside. Standing outside a ball was not the time to interrogate her charge. She gestured to Thel to follow his parents, then drew Constance aside. "Show me your dance card."

Constance fished it out of her sleeve and spread the leaves

apart. This dismay on her face would have been comical if she had not been so obviously distressed. "There are so many dances. Must I join all of them?"

Olivia stifled a laugh. She had almost forgotten the careful hand debutantes required.

"No, you mustn't. In fact..." She tapped on three lines, dispersed through the sheet. "As this is your first season, you are expected to sit these out. Use the pencil attached to the other end of the string to place an X in those spaces. Any man who asks to see the card will understand what that means."

Constance found the small nub of pencil, then frowned. "What do I do during those dances, then? I don't want to be perceived as a wallflower."

"I'll show you," Olivia said, gesturing toward the house.

They climbed the steps and stood just outside the door so Constance could see inside without being observed.

The ballroom was long and narrow, with a ceiling that went up three stories to a peak. Garlands of greenery hung from the rafters between rows of black chandeliers, burning with candles rather than gaslight.

Several tables and chairs were set up closest to them, and beyond that, women in colorful dresses swirled in the arms of suited men.

Olivia motioned toward a group of matrons gracing a table along the far wall.

Constance screwed up her face. "But they're older than my grandmother. They'll pinch my cheeks and treat me like a child."

"Exactly. No one will bother you for a dance because no one will want to come near. Now, let's not waste any more time." She drew Constance into the ballroom and pointed out the three men she had selected as initial candidates.

First was Sir Newton, newly arrived from Scotland. His copper hair and bright-green eyes made him immediately recognizable. Next was Lord Winsley, the second son of their host, the Duke of Haversham. He was more difficult to spot, but she eventually found him lurking in the shadows near the last candidate, Mr. Inwood, heir to a remarkable fortune and blessed with a softness of features that had many ladies swooning over him.

Each young man was eminently suitable, of even temper, and handsome enough to attract Constance's attention.

"What if none of them interest me?" Constance bit her lip. "What if there's… someone else?"

Olivia's heart thudded in her chest. This was her chance to extract information. She had to be careful. If she seemed too eager, too much like a parent, she might cause Constance to withdraw. She kept her tone light. "Then I would suggest you use tonight as an opportunity to test your feelings."

Constance tilted her head. "What do you mean?"

Olivia grasped for a reason the girl would follow. "Infatuation is a fleeting state, not a solid base for a marriage. Exploring other possibilities will either reveal you have settled your heart or confirm you are still uncertain."

"I suppose so," Constance said. "Well, no use waiting until I sprout roots."

They stepped into the light, and within moments, Sir Newton separated from the group of ladies he had been speaking to and headed directly toward them.

A look of utter panic filled Constance's face.

"Stay calm," Olivia whispered. "He will greet me first, as we have already been introduced. That will give you time to reassemble. If you still feel as if you cannot speak, begin with a deep curtsey."

Constance gave a shaky nod.

Sir Newton arrived. "Lady Allen. Lady Constance."

Constance answered the young man's bow with a curtsey. "Sir Newton."

Something tight inside Olivia unwound. She had worried about Constance's ability to cope with the pressure of her first official event.

"May I have your next dance?" Sir Newton asked.

Constance glanced at Olivia, then tilted her head back and returned her attention to Sir Newton. "Certainly, sir."

The girl accepted Sir Newton's hand and cast only a fleeting glance over her shoulder before the pair vanished into the swirl of dancers.

OLIVIA'S CHEEKS ACHED as she smiled and nodded along to Mr. Millwood's droning voice. Behind her, a harpist plucked a gentle melody. Each strumming note sent a throb of pain through her temple. She would have made an excuse to depart from Mr. Millwood, but her position near the musicians gave her a near-perfect view of the ballroom. As such, she was able to track Constance's movements without appearing to do so.

She reached into her pocket and flipped a worn shilling over and over in her fingers.

The repetitive motion soothed her, although it was not as effective as shifting her weight from foot to foot. That had driven her governess to distraction. It was also not something Lady Allen would have been seen doing.

Mr. Millwood turned his head as another young woman in a scandalously low-cut dress walked past them, and she took the opportunity to make her apologies and rush off before he could claim her for the next dance. Her head ached so fiercely, she was uncertain she could finish a dance without tripping over her own feet.

Not that it mattered. She had only attended to encourage Constance to socialize.

As she passed Mrs. Millwood, the woman covered her face with her fan and giggled. Her companion, a woman Olivia did not recognize, shushed her but then began giggling as well.

Their laughter was at her expense, of course. That much was

obvious. She had received many such reactions since leaving the duke's and duchess's side. Without the novelty of their presence, she became again the target of whispers, it seemed.

"Lady Allen!"

Olivia stopped, then forced a smile, even as her neck screamed in protest. She turned to see Baron and Baroness Mason. Her shoulders immediately eased. Lady Mason was one of her earliest success stories. Her match and the following wedding had been the talk of the season. Even the queen had attended and expressed her appreciation.

Except Lady Mason wasn't smiling. Her usually sparkling brown eyes were downcast and she carefully clutched her husband's arm. Despite the cloying warmth in the ballroom, she wore elbow-length white gloves and a cotton fichu embroidered with white flowers.

"Lady Allen," Lord Mason said, baring his teeth in a grin. He tugged the lapel of his red corduroy suit jacket, which barely disguised his bulging stomach. "I am heartened to see you, despite those nasty rumors." He leaned in, his dark-brown eyes meeting hers with an intensity that made her shiver. "I was a friend of the earl, and I do not believe for a moment that a mere chit such as yourself could have overwhelmed him. Those scandal rags have no shame." He patted his wife's hand on his sleeve. "Rest assured, we remain on your side."

Before she could express her thanks, the harpist behind him tipped her instrument over and it clattered to the ground with a *thud*.

Lady Mason yelped.

"Merely an accident," Lord Mason said. He tugged her closer, and for a moment, Lady Mason's glove slid down, revealing a striped pattern of bruises along her arm.

A pattern Olivia knew too well.

Cold washed over her as she remembered how her wardrobe had changed over the course of her marriage, how her favorite dresses with their delicate cap sleeves and plunging necklines had become impossible to wear. How she had set aside her fine, lace gloves in favor of silk so no one would see the marks the earl had placed upon her.

By the time Olivia had processed what she had seen, Lady Mason was gone, absorbed into the crowd with her husband.

What had gone wrong?

The last time she had seen Lady Mason, the woman had gushed about her husband. All signs had indicated she'd been in love, and her comments had suggested Lord Mason had felt the same.

Olivia made for the doors, not caring when her shoulder bumped a man's arm.

Lady Mason had expressed concerns about Lord Mason before she had walked down the aisle. She had called her betrothed "intense" and "intimidating." Having seen many young women transform from blushing brides to bundles of nerves when the altar had beckoned, Olivia had dismissed the young Miss Culter's worries and reassured her Lord Mason had been her perfect match.

She had pressed more than a dozen girls into matrimony, assured of the safety of her choices. She had never considered some of the men her girls had married were like the Earl of Allen.

How many of them had she failed? How many of them had coped the same way she had, by carefully developing a mask to use within society, to hide the truth of the abuse that occurred in their own homes?

She had almost reached the door when a hand caught her arm and forced her to a stop.

"Come with me," Thel said.

"I-I cannot," she said.

"Come with me," he repeated, and the thread of anger in his voice took her breath away. She dropped her gaze and followed demurely behind him, out of the ballroom and down a hallway. He swept her through an open door and followed behind.

Her head pounded, her mouth was dry, and she was certain

she owed apologies to half a dozen ladies for bumping them in her rush to depart the ballroom. But minor inconveniences were nothing compared to the hell Lady Mason was living.

Thel clutched her upper arms and shook her gently. "Olivia, look at me."

The movement jolted her out of her spiraling thoughts, but she couldn't face him as herself. He would surely see the evidence of her guilt. Instead, she draped her arms over his shoulders and grinned. "Is it time for a lesson in punishment?"

He frowned. "You were upset a moment ago. You looked as if you'd seen a ghost."

"A trifling matter." She pressed her lips to his in a chaste kiss.

He loosened his grip. "You don't have to do this, Olivia. You don't have to hide yourself from me."

Her seductive smile slipped. "I don't know what you mean."

He cupped her face in his hands and rubbed her cheeks with his thumbs. "I don't expect you to be perfect. God knows I have my own flaws. But I would rather have all of you than see only the parts that you feel are acceptable."

A lump formed in her throat. She tried to swallow it down, but it wouldn't budge. She opened her lips, and no sound came out.

"You can't let it go, can you?" He walked over to a daybed, tore the heavy blanket from atop it, and draped it over his shoulders. Then he walked toward her, the blanket draped around his body. When he was close enough to touch, he raised his arms.

"Come to me, Helen," he said in a gravelly voice.

His words were straight out of the story she had read in his notebook, where George comforted his wife. He was giving her an excuse to fall into a different role alongside him.

It was a temptation she could not resist.

Her eyes burned with tears before she let the character of Helen settle around her. She opened her mouth once again, and this time, words came out, rough but understandable. "Yes, husband."

Then she launched herself against his chest.

The blanket smelled musty and scratched where it touched her skin, but she didn't care. The added sensation helped drown out the guilt and anger churning within her.

He dug his fingers into her scalp and rubbed circles that sent a tingling sensation down her back. She relaxed against his body, putting more and more of her weight on him until he paused his ministrations to pick her up and carry her to a chair. Then he settled her on his lap.

She kept waiting for him to ask for whatever it was he wanted in exchange, to demand another lesson or start one without her consent. Nearly every man she had ever been intimate with had used kindness as a currency to buy sexual favors.

But he remained silent, wrapped around her like a tight-fitting glove.

"I've got you," he whispered. "Are you okay?"

She was the furthest thing from okay. His gentle words and actions stoked a furnace deep inside her and made her want to kiss him and sob in equal measure.

"You're shaking." He kissed the top of her head. "It's okay. I'm here."

She breathed in his clean soap smell until she no longer felt like she was going to explode, her muscles relaxing an inch at a time.

"There. That's better."

She knew she should return to the ball, but the emotions whirling within her were not yet settled, and her head still ached.

She plucked his cravat free and began unbuttoning his shirt.

"Are you sure?" Thel asked.

She answered by tearing at his clothes in a fury, desperate to feel his skin beneath her fingers. He stayed passive beneath her, one hand still rubbing her back.

At last, his chest was bare. She reached for the fall of his trousers.

"Not yet," he whispered. "I want you to have your pleasure first."

His words sent bolts of heat to her center. She took his right hand and slid it beneath her skirts. He smoothed his palm up her thigh until the backs of his fingers brushed her curls, his thumb tantalizingly close to her entrance. Still, he did not venture further. It was as if he were charting her, learning every curve and hollow of her body. Finally, he slid his finger around her clitoris.

She saw stars.

"There you are," he said.

He rubbed in small circles until she was moving her body into his hand, pleasure thrumming through her in a heady wave. He slipped his other hand beneath her skirts and gently, oh so gently, slid a finger inside her.

"The motion you showed me combined with penetration should…" He slid his finger out and then back in, deeper each time, until she was riding him.

A throbbing beneath her signaled he was equally excited by their actions. She reached between his legs and, with a few quick movements, freed his impressively thick cock.

He stroked himself but then stopped, his cheeks turning the same color as his engorged member.

"Continue," she said. "Show me how you pleasure yourself."

He grasped his cock, traveling all the way down before returning. He appeared to prefer a long motion, rocking his hips into it, never speeding up but continuing at an even pace, much like the way he had thrust inside her.

She touched his hand. "Allow me."

He released his grip, and she took over, copying the movement. His groans and the rocking of his hips were all the encouragement she needed.

He closed his eyes. "I cannot last long, I fear."

She grabbed his cravat from the floor, then slid her hand up and down his cock three times before he moaned. She slid the cravat over him and caught his seed, then tossed the scrap of fabric over the side of the chair.

Chapter Thirteen

THEL LEANED AGAINST the wall and watched Olivia seamlessly insert herself between two young men in the circle around Constance. In any other group, he would have expected at least a few ruffled feathers, but Olivia had a particular talent for blending in. He noticed the exact moment they switched from salivating over Olivia's beauty to assuring her of their noble intentions toward Constance.

Her ability to change how they treated her with only a few comments and a shift in her posture was remarkable. He remembered how she'd thrashed in his arms. A completely different woman from the one standing stoically beside his daughter near the door to the retiring room. What they had done was beyond anything he had ever tried with Marguerite. The few times they'd had sex before she'd fallen ill had been in total darkness and had lasted only a few minutes.

Marguerite.

He tensed, waiting for the twisting of his gut that always accompanied thoughts of his late wife, but it didn't come. His body felt light, as if a weight had slipped off his shoulders. It should have worried him, but he felt only relief that the wound Marguerite's death had left was finally healing.

He made his way through the crowd until he reached Olivia's side.

"How does she fare?" he whispered and he was pleased to see

a flush creep up from her neck.

"Constance is distracted," she said.

He turned his attention to his daughter. She lifted her chin and tilted her head from side to side, as if searching the crowd.

He did the same, even though he did not know who or what he was searching for, until he spotted a young man making his way toward them. Something about him was familiar, but it was not until he arrived at their group and bowed before Constance that he recognized the hazel eyes and slightly crooked nose of the boy who was one of Constance's earliest friends.

"I-It can't be," Constance said, her eyes wide. "What are you doing here, Sammy?"

Olivia drew closer to whisper in his ear. "Who is that, and how does she know him?"

He tilted his head so he could speak with no one hearing.

"Mr. Samuel Ringwell. Her childhood friend."

Olivia pressed close to him. "Would you be amenable to a match between them?"

Thel frowned at the grinning Samuel. The boy was high-spirited. He had once dared Constance to leap from the roof of the stable onto an enormous pile of pillows they had gathered while their nannies had been napping. He had only interrupted the foolish game by chance when he had returned home early from a spring festival in the village, sparing Constance from a broken leg, or worse.

He vaguely remembered the elder Mr. Ringwell had died in a boating accident. That meant young Sammy had some manner of wealth, although perhaps not enough to support a wife. Felix and Elijah might disapprove, but they would have difficulty finding fault in a boy they had known for years.

Olivia elbowed him in the ribs. "Well?"

"I could be persuaded," he said.

"Excellent," Olivia whispered. Then she casually inserted herself back into the conversation between Constance and Mr. Ringwell. In a matter of minutes, she had convinced Constance to join the next dance with her childhood friend.

When the music started, Thel took Olivia's hand, and they followed Mr. Ringwell and Constance.

The group split into two lines. He hooked his elbow with Olivia's and spun, kicking his heels in tune to the beat. Unlike Constance, Olivia did not allow her joy to show on her face. The small smile on her lips did not reflect in her eyes, and he caught her twisting her head around at the end of their final set. Only when they stopped and bowed to each other did he realize why.

Constance was no longer on the dance floor.

He searched for her golden head amid the sea of guests but could find neither her nor Mr. Ringwell. How had she vanished without him noticing?

Olivia clutched his arm without him offering it. "Do not make a fuss," she said. "Stroll with me. She could not have gone far."

He squeezed her hand and did as she suggested, walking fast enough that no one interrupted them, not meeting the gaze of anyone who glanced his way. To do so would be to invite discussion.

They had completed half a rotation of the room when he spotted Constance's golden head out of the corner of his eye. She stood in a dark alcove next to a disheveled man in a silver-and-black-striped jacket.

"Wait," Olivia said. "Let me talk to her first."

He glanced at Olivia, then back to his daughter. Even from a distance, he could tell she was uncomfortable. Whatever was going on couldn't be good.

Olivia squeezed his arm. "Trust me, Thel."

"I'll give you five minutes," he said, even though he felt certain Constance needed rescue, not a lecture. "As long as he doesn't put his hands on her."

Nothing would stop him from strangling any man who dared assault his daughter.

"Thank you," she said. Then she maneuvered through the

crowd toward Constance, who was suddenly alone. He searched the room but could not find the man to whom she had been speaking. When Olivia reached Constance's side, they tilted their heads together, and the tension in his shoulders eased.

Then a footman crossed his path, and when he could see Constance again, Olivia was not with her.

He shoved through the crowd as politely as he could and grasped his daughter's shoulder. "Where did Olivia go?"

"*Lady Allen* chased after the man who was talking to me. When he saw her, he ran." She pouted. "He said he had a message, but he ran before he could give it to me."

Thel suppressed the growl rising in his throat. "We will discuss this when we return home." He placed Constance's hand on his arm and kept his steps light, not wanting to attract attention, even as his instincts screamed at him that something was wrong.

They exited onto the terrace, and a chilly wind blew past, ruffling Constance's curls. She gave a quiet shriek and slapped her hands to head.

He searched the grounds until he found Olivia near a pergola. She was struggling with the man who had been speaking to Constance.

He dropped his daughter's hand and leaped down the steps three at a time, his vision focused on Olivia. He thrashed through the greenery and made it in time to find Olivia standing over a man sprawled on the ground on his stomach. The neckline of her bodice was askew, and her hair was in disarray, but otherwise, she was whole.

He itched to pull her into his arms and confirm with his hands that she had no injuries, but she was scowling and had her fists raised.

The prone man rose on his elbows. Olivia kicked him in the stomach, eliciting a moan.

"What happened?" He positioned between her and the prone man. If the bastard so much as twitched, Thel would be on him.

Olivia swept a hand along her disheveled hair. "I asked him

what he wanted with Constance. He wouldn't answer. I pressed him, and he attacked."

"He *attacked*? How did you—"

"I sought out training in how to defend myself after the late earl passed." She gulped, then looked at her hands. "He wanted Constance, Thel. Not me. What if she had followed him?"

A wave of cold washed over him. That was not a scenario he wanted to envision. He had been out of society long enough that he'd forgotten how dangerous it was for young, unmarried women. He was too used to country balls, where everyone present had known each other since birth.

He folded Olivia into his arms. Both she and Constance were safe. For the moment.

The fallen man rolled onto his back with a groan. Thel nudged Olivia behind him and crouched down to get a better look at her attacker's face. "What was your plan?"

The man curled his lip. "Don't believe that lying chit. She led me out here, said she'd let me lift her skirts if I was quick about it."

"Check his pockets," Olivia said. "Constance said he had a message."

Thel was already rooting through the man's jacket. He found a ribbon-wrapped envelope and held it up. Olivia grabbed it and tore it open.

The man jackknifed his legs and swiped a gloved hand at her legs, but she neatly danced out of the way.

Thel put his hand on the man's neck and thrust him against the ground. "That's enough from you, unless you'd like to add a broken back to the list of your injuries." He glanced at Olivia. "What is it?"

She slipped the envelope into her pocket. "A problem."

Chapter Fourteen

Dearest Constance,

Please forgive this unorthodox method of communication, but time is of the essence. I presented what we gathered so far to my creditors, but they were not willing to release me from my commitments. If your pin money is insufficient, perhaps there are objects in that house you could sell—statues or paintings gathering dust in dark corners that no one will miss.

Sincerely,
D

"WHERE DID YOU meet this man?" Thel asked.

His daughter curled into the corner of the carriage, her arms crossed, her neck turned toward the window. Olivia sat beside her, chewing her lower lip between her teeth. Constance had not said a word since he had presented her with the letter they had taken from Olivia's attacker. When faced with the prospect of being turned over to the Scotland Yard, the man had confessed that an unknown party had paid him to deliver the note.

He'd been unable to give any more information, but Thel was certain the incident was related to the lack of funds in Constance's account and the letters they'd found in her room.

"How much have you given him?" he asked.

Constance tucked her chin to her chest. "It was my money to

give away. John needed it."

"John who?" Olivia asked. "Do you even know his last name?"

"Of course I do!"

Olivia hummed a sound that was both noncommittal and patronizing.

Constance turned back to the window. "If you must know, his name is John Dawson. I met him in the village." She cupped her cheek in her hand and continued in a softer voice. "It was the night of the summer festival. I waited for Mrs. Quill to be distracted before slipping away to watch the dancing. Then a handsome man approached me and held out a handkerchief he'd picked up, asking if I'd dropped it. It was so sweet of him to ask, even though it wasn't mine." She gave a dreamy sigh. "Oh, John."

Thel had never heard of the man, and his daughter's omission of a "Sir" or "Lord" meant he was untitled.

"You might have told me you had a suitor before I engaged a matchmaker," he said, taking great care to keep his tone level. It was embarrassing enough having Olivia in the carriage with them without resorting to shouting.

"John said you wouldn't understand." Constance pursed her lips. "He was right."

He kept his response to himself. Events were occurring exactly as Olivia had predicted. It followed that an angry outburst from him would have the effect she had described, chasing his daughter further into *Dawson's* arms.

"He only needs my help for a few more months," Constance said. "He'll have more than enough money once his inheritance comes through. His father owned a rail company in America before he died."

Thel was doubtful. A man who begged a woman for money, especially in such large amounts, was not a man who could be trusted to maintain a fortune. Every pound he swindled out of Constance was likely reinvested in the local pub.

The carriage rocked back and forth, the sound of footfalls and horse hooves coming from outside as they made their slow way through the crowded streets. Thel kept one hand near the door, fearing that the mysterious Dawson would throw it open and steal Constance away.

A foolish thought. If Dawson wanted to marry Constance, there were far easier ways to force her hand. They had only to look at young Miss Perry, who had been caught kissing Mr. Rutledge behind the rose bushes last season. Witnesses reported that the young bride had to be forced down the aisle by her parents, sobbing all the while.

The carriage slowed to a stop, and a footman opened the door. Constance flew down the steps and into their home like a blur. Thel stepped out and offered Olivia his arm, which she took. He clutched her close, and she did not complain even when she had to pause at the bottom of the steps for him to release her.

They entered the house, and she followed him to his office. He sulked to his desk and threw himself into his chair.

A servant rushed inside and prepared the fire while Olivia perched in the chair opposite him.

He had only been in London a fortnight. How had his life become so complicated so quickly?

The servant finished setting the fire and rushed out of the room, slipping on the floor in his rush to depart.

"We have to cut off Constance's contact with this man," he said.

Olivia shook her head. "She would never forgive you."

She sounded so certain, and she'd been right about Constance being in contact with a man. Still, this was his daughter.

"How do you know?" he asked.

"Because that is what my father tried to do to me."

All the anger flowed out of him. "Your father did not want you to marry the Earl of Allen?"

"Not at first," she said. "My mother had hoped to use my family's fortune to entice a duke or marquess, not a 'mere' earl. When they discovered the letters the earl had sent me, they accused me of ruining myself." She smoothed her palms over the waist of her gown. "They were wrong. When we first met, the earl was adamant that we could only ever be friends. No unmarried man had ever told me that."

"He made himself forbidden," Thel said. It was a story as old as time.

"Yes. I could not resist falling for the one man I could not have. I believe that is how Mr. Dawson got to Constance."

It was horrifying knowing his daughter was being manipulated and frustrating because there was so little he could do.

Olivia stood and paced the room. "There's still something I don't understand. If Mr. Dawson is motivated by revenge against me, marrying Constance would not accomplish that goal, unless he made it known I had failed in my duties by allowing him to ruin her, but if that were his only goal, he would have done so already." She grimaced. "It is easy to force a young woman into a compromising position. There must be something else Mr. Dawson wants that he cannot get through marriage alone. I just don't know what, or how he's connected to the former earl."

Thel thumped back in his chair. "There must be something we can do."

If he had been willing to let Constance marry any man who was only interested in her dowry, he would have allowed Felix to select a husband for her. At least then she would have had the comfort of a title.

"How did you end up married to the earl?" he asked. "If Dawson is following the same pattern, maybe there is a clue in your past to how to stop this."

Olivia pulled off her glove and stuck her thumbnail in her mouth. "When I told my parents the earl and I were only friends, they didn't believe me. They demanded I marry the earl immediately. I refused." She laughed. "I had convinced myself the earl didn't want me, and I loved him too much to force him."

Thel could imagine her, a much younger woman, standing stubbornly before her furious father. A shudder passed through him. If Olivia had not told him to heel, he had no doubt his own confrontation with Constance would have gone the same way.

"My parents kept me locked in the house as punishment," Olivia continued. "When the earl found out, he got one of our maids to deliver a letter saying he would marry me if it would rescue me from my parents." She sighed. "If Constance feels for Mr. Dawson the way I did for the earl, then she won't give up on him."

The truth of her words resonated with him and infuriated him in equal measure. He had initially hoped that by introducing Constance to society early, they would have plenty of time to find her perfect match. Instead, he had catapulted them into disaster.

Then a thought struck him. "What could your father have done to separate you and the earl before it was too late?"

Olivia frowned. "That is an excellent question. Perhaps if more time had passed. The earl acted on his best behavior for the few days we officially courted, but he could not have kept it up for long. If I had seen his true personality before we married, it might have been enough to shake my faith." She paced the room. "What if we encouraged Mr. Dawson to court her?"

"You cannot be serious."

He was of the opinion that they leave the city immediately. A few months away from Dawson would surely rid Constance of her infatuation.

Olivia stopped at the window and drew her finger along the condensation, forming a heart before crossing it out. "This is my fault. If it weren't for me, he might never have targeted Constance. Now that he has her in his grasp, I worry he won't let her go."

The sadness and grief in her voice made him want to squeeze her tightly and protect her from the prying eyes of society.

The realization that he cared for her, truly cared for her, rocked him, and he saw, for the first time, the danger in their arrangement. If he allowed his feelings to grow, parting from her would scar his already bruised heart. They could have no future together. He had found and lost his one true love.

Unless God was giving him a second chance.

A fluttering started in his stomach and rose to his throat before he swallowed it down. He was getting ahead of himself. He didn't even know how Olivia felt. For all he knew, she considered him nothing more than a temporary liaison. Asking for more than that to which they had committed might very well cause her to end their relationship.

No. He would not act until he was certain his feelings were reciprocated.

He came up behind her and wrapped his arms around her waist. "I don't blame you."

She leaned back. "You don't understand. I've put you in a terrible position. If you overtly approve of Mr. Dawson, she'll use that to overlook any flaws she sees. But if you make Mr. Dawson forbidden, as the earl and my father did to me, then he'll become much more tempting. If we are to separate them, you must play a careful game of neither encouragement nor disapproval. Can you do that?"

It did sound complicated, but he would not abandon his daughter without a fight.

"I will try."

A tap came at the door, and they quickly separated before it creaked open. "Your daughter wishes to speak with you, my lord," Mrs. Quill said.

Constance stepped into the room with her head bowed. "I'm sorry I didn't tell you about John sooner."

Thel's heart ached. Why couldn't life be as simple as one of his stories? The conflict in them never lasted more than a few days before the characters reconciled and lived happily ever after. He wanted to sweep his daughter into his arms and chase her troubles away. At the same time, his coddling might have brought about her duplicity. All her life, she had come to him with her problems. Until now.

It was time she faced the consequences of her actions.

"Is that all?" he asked.

Mrs. Quill cleared her throat.

Constance wrapped her arms around herself. "He said he needed more money. He said you would never find out."

Mrs. Quill tutted. "The girl has given this daft man most of her jewels."

A pit opened in Thel's stomach. He had done wrong by his daughter, insulating her from the world when he should have been educating her about evil men.

The future unfolded in his mind in horrifying detail. Constance would marry Mr. Dawson. Furious that he'd not gotten his way, Felix would leave the house, taking Thel's nieces and nephews with him. Elijah would follow soon after, having no reason to remain.

He could not allow it to happen. Even if it caused a split between them, even if it wasn't exactly what Olivia had suggested, he had to stop Constance from starting the chain of events that would lead to him being left alone again. "I thought better of you, Connie."

"Thel. Don't," Olivia said, before he spoke over her.

"Lock her in her room."

Constance let out a sob before running away, with Mrs. Quill following. As the door slammed shut, Olivia spun around. "What was that?"

Thel ran a hand through his hair. "I-I don't know. I panicked."

How could he explain that the very idea of living by himself terrified him? A highly independent woman like her would never understand.

She heaved a sigh. "Well, the damage is done. I will see what I can do to prevent this from getting any worse."

There was nothing he felt he could say to that, so he only watched with a growing sense of desperation as she turned and walked away from him.

MRS. QUILL OPENED Constance's door at Olivia's gentle knock. The maid's fair hair fell around her face and there were bags under her eyes.

"How is she?" Olivia asked.

"She cries," Mrs. Quill said.

"Let me speak with her."

Thel might not have seen it, because his life had been blessed in comparison, but she knew what it was like to be involved with a man who was an expert at strumming the strings of her heart. She knew the ecstasy that resulted from pleasing her manipulator, and the devastation that came from failure.

"Yes, my lady," Mrs. Quill said, opening the door.

The curtains were drawn tight, with only a sliver of sunlight passing through, and the fireplace was cold. The room smelled of beeswax, originating from a stub of a candle burning on Constance's writing desk next to a stack of papers and a pen.

Constance lay on her bed with her hair loose, wearing only her chemise.

As Mrs. Quill slipped out of the room and shut the door, Olivia approached the desk. She touched a half-written letter, which was unsurprisingly addressed to Mr. Dawson.

"Father hates me," Constance said.

Olivia sat on the edge of the bed and put a hand on Constance's back. Her heart ached at the familiar scene. There had been no one to comfort her when she had sobbed after the earl had dismissed her with words of anger.

When Constance's sobs quieted, Olivia crawled onto the bed beside her and leaned into the headboard. "You might not believe it, but I was once a girl on the cusp of womanhood, as you are."

Constance sniffed. "A hundred years ago."

Olivia made a mock sound of outrage. "How old do you think I am?"

"Sorry. Is this the story of how you met Lord Allen?"

"It is. Although it is probably not the romance you are expecting. When I met Lord Allen, he was a much older man who was adamant that we could never be anything but friends. Despite that, I quickly grew to care for him because he was the only person who listened to me. Who treated me like an adult."

The transition from friendship to infatuation had happened quickly. One day she'd been telling him about her frustrations with her parents, the next, she'd been daydreaming about becoming the Countess of Allen.

"After I admitted I held feelings for him, he changed. He told me the most beautiful things. That I was his true love. That he could not bear to be parted from me."

She chuckled. She had only discovered later he had cribbed the poems from old archives instead of creating them himself. The earl had been like that, expending the minimum effort to achieve his goals. He'd preferred to convince others to do his bidding than to dirty his own hands.

"When we finally married, I was so happy. The earl was a perfect husband. He showered me with love and affection." She paused, remembering the moment her world had turned upside down. "As long as I was the perfect wife in return."

She recalled the day she had finally realized how badly she had erred. It had been the day after he had locked her in her bedchamber for the first time, because she'd dared to wear a gown other than the one he had selected. It had scared her so badly that she'd sobbed for hours, trying to reconcile the shouting, angry man with the man she had married.

Only her elderly butler, Boris, had dared to bring her food when the earl had been in a temper. All the other servants had been terrified of the earl and what he would do to them if they'd tried to help her.

Then the earl had died, and it had felt as if a thousand heavy chains had slipped off her shoulders. She'd maintained the strictest of mourning rituals for the required two years, and then slowly, ever so slowly, had emerged as something new.

Lady Allen. Countess Dowager. Flirtatious, enterprising, clever. A woman every lady wanted in attendance at her events and every man desired in his bed. The most successful role she'd ever played.

Constance slid her hand into Olivia's and squeezed. "I'm sorry he died."

Olivia sighed. "I'm not. He was a cruel man. Marrying him was the worst mistake I ever made." Now was her chance to connect her story back to Mr. Dawson, although if Constance had not caught the connection yet, then the girl might never understand. "What if Mr. Dawson is the same as the earl? What if he turns into the worst mistake of your life?"

Constance stiffened and curled into a tighter ball. "John isn't like that."

Olivia sighed. The girl was not yet ready to hear the truth. That meant her best option was to negotiate.

"A test, then," she said. "To confirm he truly is the man you say he is."

Constance uncurled and looked up with her bright eyes, her eyebrows furrowed. "What kind of test?"

Olivia's mind raced. How could she tempt Dawson into revealing himself without putting the girl in actual danger? It had to be something Dawson would believe Constance had thought up herself.

She tried to remember how she had felt about the earl during the early days of their courtship. She had been so desperate for approval that she had made long lists of the earl's strengths and shared them with anyone who would listen.

Olivia could not side with Constance without risking setting her against her father, but she could use the girl's desperation against her.

"A man who truly loves you would not marry you if you did not want to, correct?"

Constance scrunched her nose. "But I *do* want to marry him."

"I recommend you tell him you want to wait until you are older to marry. That you want a longer courtship. If he agrees, then you will know he is a true gentleman."

"And if he disagrees?"

Olivia shrugged. "Then he is not the man you think he is."

Constance was silent for a long time. At last, she spoke in a whisper. "What if he doubts my commitment? I don't want to lose him."

"Would you truly want a man who would be chased away by something so simple as waiting for marriage?" She nudged Constance in the ribs with her elbow. "Your first season should be fun, not stressful."

"I wouldn't want to ask for something so important in a letter," Constance said. "I'll need a chance to speak to him in private. At home, I was able to sneak out of my room at night, but here, Mrs. Quill is always watching."

Olivia pretended to consider this problem, so as not to give away her excitement. "Well, Mrs. Quill won't be a problem if you arrange to meet at an event. I suppose I could distract your father."

Constance's mouth dropped open. "You would do that?"

"As long as you promise to be careful."

"Of course I will." Constance bounced on her bed. Then she scrambled off and ran to her writing desk. "Which event are we going to next?"

Olivia wanted to ask how Constance's letter would reach its destination, if the girl knew where Mr. Dawson was staying, or if someone was helping them communicate, but Constance had already revealed more than Olivia had expected. She would attempt further questioning later rather than risk damaging the trust she had gained with the girl. "I thought Lord and Lady Wintermoor's masquerade." She doubted Mr. Dawson could secure a proper invitation, but a masquerade would be easy for him to sneak into.

Constance tapped her toes and squealed. "You are the best

matchmaker, Lady Allen. I was worried I wouldn't get many chances to see him. I'm going to write to him right now and I'll let you know as soon as he responds, but I'm sure he'll agree. He's always asking me to arrange opportunities for us to meet."

The admission made Olivia's skin crawl. Everything Constance had told her suggested that Mr. Dawson shared the same unsettling obsession for Constance that the earl had had for her.

She could only hope that, given time, Constance would see that, too.

Chapter Fifteen

W HEN OLIVIA LEFT Constance's room, Thel was leaning against the wall next to an open window, his arms crossed.

"How is she?" he asked.

She did not have enough of the anger she had carried earlier to respond how she wished she could. "She is confused. Lost. It will take some time for her to understand what is happening. Until then, she'll need guidance." She put her hands on her hips. "And not from you."

He ran his hand through his hair. "Being the head of this family is challenging. Our living arrangement is unusual. We all must compromise, and the situation with Constance is making it difficult to maintain harmony."

She was tempted to tell him about the deal she had made with Constance, but his refusal to listen to her earlier made her wonder if he was more like her former husband than she'd realized, hiding aspects of his personality. What if there was a cruel streak beneath his gentle exterior? She had not known him for long, and she had a history of seeing only what she wanted to see in men.

"Is that all that matters to you?" she asked. "Your family staying together?"

He frowned. "Of course. Nothing is more important."

It was a perspective she did not share. Her parents had certainly not cared about her well-being. Her mother had thrust her into the care of strangers from the moment she'd been born, from wet-nurse to nanny to governess. That might not have been so terrible, except the women who'd filled those roles had cycled out often enough that she had never had time to grow attached. There had never been any visits from aunts or uncles, no cousins with whom to play, no grandparents to bounce her on their knees.

Thel's family could not have been more different.

"My lord!" a voice called.

It was Thel's butler, walking quickly toward them.

"What is it?" Thel asked.

"A constable has arrived," the man said.

"What does he want?" Olivia asked. The words came out squeakier than she'd intended.

She remembered the uniformed man who had come to the house after the earl's death. He had demanded she account for her activities during the earl's final days, challenged every statement she'd made, and accused her of being hysterical when she'd demanded he leave. She had no desire to experience that level of disrespect again.

"Send him to the drawing room," Thel said.

As the butler left, Thel put his hands on her shoulders. Only then did she realize her hands were shaking.

"I'm overreacting," she said.

The constable probably wanted to record her statement regarding the man who had attacked her at the ball. She'd read enough detective novels to know the police always questioned the victim first, while the incident was fresh in their mind. The longer one waited to interrogate a witness, the more likely their fears were to transform meaningless details into nefarious portents. A slight rustle in the trees became a sign of a pursuer approaching, the earthy smell of moss became an odor of decay. The click of a lock engaging became the fall of a hammer in a pistol, pressed against the back of her head.

She shuddered. It had taken months of introspection to separate fact from fiction in her own memories and silence the voice in her mind that insisted she should have fought harder or screamed louder.

"I could send him away," Thel said.

She stepped closer and allowed him to wrap her in his arms. The strength of his embrace chased the ghosts of her past away and allowed her to think clearly once again. She could not retreat from the constable. It would make her look guilty.

She gathered the shreds of her control and lifted her chin. "I'll talk to him."

OLIVIA BREATHED IN the gentle scent of mint rising from the delicate, porcelain cup, then took a sip. The hot liquid soothed the inside of her cheeks, sore from constant chewing. The constable sat across from them, holding a matching cup in both hands. He wore a domed hat and a brown uniform, with a black stick and a whistle hanging from his leather belt. He was a young man, hardly older than Constance, and his face bristled with the beginning of a beard.

"I apologize again," the man, who had identified himself as Mr. Daniel Smith, said. He drank from the teacup and then picked up a scone and bit into it, scattering crumbs onto his uniform and the floor. "Procedure, you understand."

"Of course," Olivia said automatically, even as she wondered why Mr. Smith was not behaving the way the detectives in her stories did. He was far too nice, given the crime. Perhaps Constance's attacker had confessed, and Mr. Smith had been sent to deliver the good news.

The constable withdrew a leatherbound pad, flipped it open, then looked at her. "What is your relationship with your attacker, Lady Allen?"

Relationship?

That was an odd way of putting it.

"I had never met him before tonight," she said.

Mr. Smith plucked a pencil from his pocket and scribbled something down. "You confess to meeting him tonight?"

She didn't like the way he'd phrased that. Judging from Thel's scowl, he felt the same.

The interrogation, if that was what it was, was not proceeding the way she'd expected. Tricking a suspect into confessing was a common tactic but was usually prefaced by far more probing questions.

"He was speaking to Lord Lowell's daughter," she said. "When I approached, he quickly departed. I chased after and upon catching up to him, the man assaulted me."

Mr. Smith held up a hand. "Lady Allen, I believe we are referring to different matters. This man who assaulted you tonight, is he the same person who has accused you of murder?"

Her mouth went dry. "What?"

Suddenly, she understood. He had been trying to lull her into a false sense of security before dropping the revelation to gauge her reaction.

He'd succeeded.

"Mr. Smith, why are you here?" Thel asked. "Lady Allen's attacker is already on his way to jail. There is no doubt of his guilt."

The constable closed his book. "My lord, this does not concern you. I am here to investigate the claims presented against Lady Allen regarding the death of the previous Earl of Allen."

"Preposterous," Thel said before she shot him a warning glance.

"I'm afraid you are wasting your time, Mr. Smith," she said. "My husband died of consumption."

The constable narrowed his eyes. "A witness has come forward who says otherwise."

A cold bead of sweat went down her spine. That was impossible. No one else had been in the room when the earl had passed. She had seen to that herself.

Thel clasped his hands between his knees. "Have you considered this witness is only interested in the attention an investigation will stir up?"

"The thought has crossed my mind." He shoved the rest of his scone in his mouth and chewed noisily. "The editor of the *London Evening Standard* admitted to offering a hefty sum to anyone who might provide proof of misdeeds on Lady Allen's part."

The conniving bastard. It was no wonder he was not interested in helping her. He had a larger payout in mind.

Thel made a subtle gesture. A few seconds later, a servant rushed into the room with another tray and placed it on the table.

"What does this witness claim happened?" Thel asked.

"I shouldn't reveal details of the investigation," Mr. Smith said. He reached for a small cake but hesitated before his fingers touched it.

Thel pushed the tray toward the other man. "Does the accused not have a right to know the charges leveled against her?"

Olivia looked from Thel to the constable and back several times. Thel's tone was light, his posture relaxed, but a muscle in his jaw worked and his hand on the couch was clenched into a fist. When she finally realized what was happening, she wanted to smack herself. Thel was trying to gather information from the constable, and all she was doing was sitting on her rear.

She adopted her friendliest smile and leaned forward to best display her bosom. "I imagine they claimed I poisoned him?"

"That would be the sum of it," Mr. Smith said between bites.

Thel tapped her foot with his, and she forced a laugh. "Terribly unoriginal, repeating what has already been posted in the newspaper. I apologize that you've wasted your valuable time on this."

The constable brushed crumbs from his coat. "Can't say it's the first time. But original or not, I'm bound to investigate."

"We would expect nothing less," Thel said.

The constable devoured three more sweets before taking his leave.

Olivia remained in her spot as Thel guided the man to the door, her heart and thoughts racing. It was too convenient that there would be one man accusing her of murder in the newspaper, and another bringing evidence against her to the police. It had to be Mr. Dawson, attempting to separate her from her wealth. But why, and how was he associated with her late husband?

Thel returned and walked to her chair but did not touch her, to her relief. Her body felt as if it were full of buzzing insects, and it was only her tight grip on the arms of her chair that kept her from flitting around the room.

"What is it?" Thel asked.

"It's Mr. Dawson," she said. "It must be. He brought the constable here."

"I'll call him out," Thel said. "We'll settle this with a duel."

A surprised laugh bubbled out of her throat. "No, absolutely not. What reason would you give? You are not my father, brother, or husband. His attacks against my honor are not yours to defend."

Putting aside the risk that Thel might be mortally wounded, she wanted Mr. Dawson to experience the same shame and fear she had felt. A quick death would not guarantee that. She wanted assurances he would never bother Constance, or any other young woman, ever again.

More than anything, she wanted to know what she had done to elicit his ire.

"I know what I have to do," she said, the words popping out of her mouth before she realized she was speaking. She didn't want to finish her thought because she knew where it led, but she had to know the truth, and there was only one way to get to the source of the information Mr. Dawson was using against her.

It was time to return to her marital home.

Chapter Sixteen

ACCUSED MURDERESS UNDER INVESTIGATION. I am pleased to report that a constable was spotted outside Lord Lowell's residence, where Lady Allen has recently taken up visiting. We must hope London's finest have seen the error of their ways and Lady Allen will come to justice at last.

O LIVIA CLENCHED HER fingers on Thel's arm as they strolled up the stone path to the house where she had once lived. A house which now belonged to her late husband's cousin, the new Earl of Allen. She'd only met the man once, briefly, although he'd been kind enough to send a letter before he'd left to travel the Continent, informing her that she could visit the house whenever she wished.

She remembered dancing across the brown-and-white tiles in the entryway beneath the twinkling, silver chandelier, with the earl following behind. That innocent girl would never have expected she would become a prisoner in her own home, that she would spend countless evenings peering out her foggy, hexagonal bedroom windows, wishing she were anywhere else.

"It is only a house," Thel said.

He was right, but that did little to ease the ache that had started in the back of her throat. It was as if all the screams she had swallowed throughout her marriage were clamoring to escape now that the earl was not present to take pleasure in her pain.

She lifted one trembling leg and then another until she was standing in front of the old, oak door with its rusty hinges and carving of a phoenix in flight. She had always hated that bird, with its crooked beak and sightless, black eyes.

Thel smoothed a hand down her back. "Are you ready?"

She took a deep breath, then nodded.

He turned the knob and pushed. The door opened on a long creak, revealing a dimly lit interior. All of the furnishings in the foyer were covered in white sheets, and there were squares of dark patches on the walls where paintings had once rested. Where the gardens and façade had been painfully familiar, there was little she recognized inside the house.

An elderly servant in a blue tweed jacket rose from his place on a chair beneath the staircase and squinted at her. "Lady Allen?"

"Boris!" She rushed forward to greet the man who had been her only ally in a home that had sapped every ounce of life from her. "I suppose I should not be surprised to see you here. Did the new earl keep you on as butler?"

She'd wanted to ask Boris to come work for her after the funeral, but he'd been employed by her late husband's family for decades.

The old man rubbed his long beard. "That he did, my lady, although I think it was more out of convenience than tradition. Two days after the funeral, he walked through the house once, dismissed half the staff, and departed for France. But now you are here! The earl left instructions that you were to be welcome whenever you wished."

She did not have the heart to tell him she would not be visiting again. If she'd harbored any hope of convincing Boris to leave with her, she would have offered him a position in her household, but the man was far too loyal. She thanked Boris, then took Thel's hand and led him to the stairs.

Her feet moved without her bidding them. How many times had she walked down the hallway, practicing the perfect stroll, checking her face in the mirrors to confirm not a hint of what she felt shone through? The earl had encouraged this in his own way. When she showed a rare smile or hearty laugh, he would apologize for his "energetic" wife. That was when he was not calling her "youthful" and "naïve."

"My lady, you should stay out of that room," a young voice said.

She turned to see a maid twisting her apron in her hands.

"What's your name?" Olivia asked.

The girl bobbed a curtsey. "Willow, my lady. I was a maid here before you left. This room... It hasn't been prepared. It wouldn't be right for you to see it in such condition until we..." She gulped. "Until we gave it a proper cleaning."

"The condition of the room does not matter, as I'm not here to stay. This is no longer my home, Willow."

"Have you come—is there something you seek?" The quick glances Willow shot at Thel suggested there was more going on, but Olivia did not have a frame of reference to determine what it might be.

"Is something the matter?"

The maid clutched her apron in both hands, then spoke so quickly that Olivia almost didn't make out the words. "We didn't think you would mind, milady, seeing as all your possessions were moved after the old earl died, and we knew the dress wasn't yours, so Delilah sewed up the cuts in the gold chiffon and fixed the fine lace and found a buyer in the shops in Whitechapel and sold it. Begging your pardon, but the money is long gone."

Olivia shook her head. "I didn't leave any gowns behind."

Willow's gaze dropped to the floor. "I know, milady. It was the other lady. She wore it whenever she visited."

"What other lady?" she asked, but then she knew. It should not have come as a surprise. The earl had treated her no better than a possession. Of course, he had sought his pleasure with another woman.

She had come to the house determined to learn where her

nemesis was getting information, but now it was obvious. It was not a member of her staff at all, but her former husband's mistress.

She forced her attention back to Willow. The girl was speaking even faster and with such a high-pitched voice that Olivia feared she was on the verge of faint.

"...swore us to silence, and even after he died, we feared his old ghost would haunt the place."

"You aren't in trouble, Willow," she said. "Can you tell me more about..." She had to force the words out. "This woman. What did she look like?"

Thel might have called her masochistic for delving so deep into the earl's sins, but any woman who'd willingly come to the earl's bed had to have been lacking in both self-preservation and morality. Exactly the kind of woman who would be amenable to bribes.

Willow ducked her head. "I wish I could tell you more, but the previous earl was very careful when his mistress was concerned. I think he didn't like us knowing what he was up to. I only ever caught glimpses of her."

She looked so anxious that Olivia felt compelled to smile. "You can return to your duties, Willow."

As the girl hurried away, Thel threaded his fingers through hers and squeezed. "Do you feel this woman is important?"

"Yes."

The earl had taken pleasure in sharing the secrets he had extracted out of his acquaintances with her, especially when said information made her uncomfortable. He had once gleefully informed her that Lady Cowper had been beaten by her husband so badly that she could not exit her house without wearing a veil.

If he had continued the practice of sharing secrets with his mistress, then the lady was likely in possession of many unpleasant facts.

Facts Mr. Dawson could use against me.

But how were Mr. Dawson and her husband's mistress connected? Her first thought was they were lovers, although she had to admit her own history guided her in that direction. It was equally possible that they were related or were strangers who had formed a partnership to enact revenge against her. She still didn't know what she had done to elicit Mr. Dawson's anger, but she could easily imagine the earl's mistress resenting the wife of her deceased lover. "Are you certain you wish to do this?" Thel asked. "You might find the past holds answers to questions you did not ask."

"I have to know," she said. "It's the only way we'll get to the truth."

He released her. "If that is what you want. How do we find this woman?"

Olivia chewed on her thumbnail through her glove. "The earl was careful with the staff. He wouldn't have allowed any of them to overhear the manner of things that have come to light in the articles. Except..." There was only one person the earl had consistently treated with respect. The oldest servant in their employ. "Boris."

Thel frowned. "That old man?"

"He's worked for my late husband's family for decades. He often said he helped raise the previous earl."

"You think he might have seen something?"

Before he had finished his sentence, she was flying down the steps, her heart thudding in her chest. "Boris!"

He was back in his chair, although there was a new black cane clenched in his hands. "Yes, my lady?"

She knelt before him. "Do you remember how you would bring food to my room?"

He tapped his cane on the tile. "My memory is not that bad, my lady. You were a wee thing, barely more than skin and bones. The previous earl did wrong by you."

"Yes, of course, but on those nights, did a woman come to the house?"

Boris's expression glazed over. "A woman... Yes, there was a woman. I told the daft boy he was getting himself into trouble, having an affair with a married lady, but he was never one to listen to sense. The same as his father, that boy."

Olivia felt as if someone had punched her in the gut. It was bad enough that her husband had sought the company of another, but she had assumed his liaisons had been with actresses or ballerinas or maybe even ladies of the night, not a woman of her own class.

"You are certain she was a lady?" Thel asked.

Boris's eyebrows drew together. "I only saw her once in passing, my lord, but she must have been a lady, because she was with Miss Trenton. That viper of a woman would not have associated with anyone of lower class."

"Trenton," Olivia said, drawing out the word. "I know that name." Then it came to her, and she groaned. "Mrs. Zephyr was Miss Trenton before she married."

She would have more luck getting a tiger to come placidly to her hand than convincing that woman to help her identify the former earl's mistress. She had come so far, torn open long-healed wounds, all for nothing.

It was too much. She wanted out of the house, away from the memories that choked her on every corner. The earl had never truly left, only hid in the recesses of her mind. She could hear his distant shouting, feel his lips upon her breast, taste the alcohol on his breath when he'd forced his tongue into her mouth.

She balled her hands into fists. The earl would not win.

She dragged Thel back upstairs and into the bedroom that had been her prison during her marriage, then slammed and locked the door behind them.

"What are you doing?" Thel asked.

She knelt over to unlace her boot. "Facing my demons."

She removed her other boot, then walked to the bed and flipped up the velvet-lined loops the earl had once used to make her debase herself, furthering his pleasure from her humiliation.

"Are those…?" Thel trailed off. "They are. My God."

MENTOR TO THE MARQUESS

She still had nightmares about using the loops. It infuriated her that the earl continued to affect her after his death. If she was ever to be free of him, she had to confront her memories head-on and reclaim what he had taken from her.

She stuck her wrists in the loops and tightened them as best she could. There was enough slack that her arms were not stretched taut. If she scooted down on the bed, she could lie with her arms slightly above her head.

"Lash my ankles," she said.

Thel stared at her for so long, she worried he had not heard, but then he flipped the loops from beneath the mattress and closed them around her ankles, pulling them until she had a few inches of movement.

"What now?" Thel asked.

"Blindfold me with your cravat."

Thel jerked off his neckcloth and held it in his hands. "Are you sure?"

She wasn't, but she had to do something. She couldn't allow the earl to haunt her every waking hour.

"I need this, Thel. It's the only way I'll be able to forget what happened here."

He crawled across the bed and draped the fabric over her face, then tied it behind her head. It wasn't enough to obscure her vision, but being unable to see made her more attuned to the sounds in the room. She felt the dip of the bed as he crawled onto it.

Her heart raced. The anticipation was as sweet as any kiss. She wanted to be entirely filled with him, with his tongue and his fingers and his cock.

When his chilled fingers touched her ankle, she jerked. But he only caressed her foot, then took her big toe in his mouth and sucked. A jolt of lust shot through her. He lifted her skirts and trailed kisses to her quim, then peeled her apart layer by layer. He rasped her clitoris, curling his tongue around it in a movement that had her hips rocking.

"More," Olivia whispered.

He pressed his fingers between her nether lips and pierced her in one swift movement. She rocked her hips with the rapid thrust of his fingers, riding him until she was lathered in sweat.

"Take me, Thel," she said. "Claim me."

His fingers vanished, and she cried out for need of him, but then something broad and smooth pressed between her thighs. She nudged as far down as she could, but he remained tantalizingly against her entrance.

He pushed in a fraction, just enough for him to feel his fullness entering her, stretching her tight. She squirmed on his cock, trying to take more of him, but he held her hips down onto the bed and slid in another fraction.

He was so big. He stretched her more than any man ever had, inch by tortuous inch, until he lifted her hips and pulled her the rest of the way. She tried to wrap her legs around his waist, but they snagged on the restraints.

She wanted him to move, to take her until she could think of nothing else. Instead, he drew himself back as slowly as he had entered her. When he was nearly out, he plunged back in. She thrashed her head back and forth, panting. She loved having him so deep. Being at his mercy.

"Please," she said.

He filled her so deep, and she could do nothing but take it as pinned as she was. She clung to the sensation of him inside her, tightening the muscles in her abdomen to make the sensation that much sweeter. Still, it was not enough.

"What do you need?" he whispered.

Tension coiled in her abdomen but would not come free. It happened sometimes, when her mind was not engaged, like she was floating above herself rather than inside her body.

"Use your mouth," she said.

Her sex dampened as he pressed gentle kisses along her clavicle. His beard rubbed against her sensitive flesh and made her back arch. He tugged the top of her gown and her corset down and touched his lips to her nipple through her shift, then drew back on a gasp.

"Yes, it's what you think," she said. "They are even more sensitive this way."

Thel probed her with his tongue, exploring one of the many holes pierced through her anatomy. It was one of the few wounds the earl had given her she was not ashamed of.

There were several interesting things one could do with bosom rings and chains that enhanced pleasure.

She looked forward to introducing Thel to all of them.

At last, she unwound around him with a sigh, the pleasure coursing up her back and curling in her belly.

THEL'S VISION WENT white as Olivia's sheath fluttered around his cock. He had intended to hold on to his release, but the evidence of her pleasure tipped him over the edge. He thrust deep and spent himself, then rode the waves of pleasure along with her.

Several minutes later, he slipped out of her and untied her restraints. She immediately curled against him, laying her head on his chest and splaying one leg across his hips.

"That was...remarkable," he said.

Her laugh was hardly more than a soft exhalation. "My dear marquess, we have only begun."

He was grateful. While they continued in their pursuits, she remained in his orbit. He felt more confident than ever that he had been given a second chance at love, and he would not let it pass him by. After what they'd done, she might become pregnant with his heir. There was only one logical path forward.

He wrapped his arms around her. "We could spend every morning like this."

She snorted. "I do have my own household, Thel. After this matter of the articles is resolved, I will have a life to return to. It would be rather difficult to maintain a social presence if I am always traveling between your house and mine."

He splayed his hand on her stomach. "That was not precisely what I had in mind."

"Then what?"

"You could be my wife."

She squirmed out of bed, taking the blanket with her. "Are you in love with me?"

He could not see her face or read her intentions from her tone. It left him scrambling. "Marriages have been established on shakier ground. We are compatible. We enjoy each other's company." He slid off the bed and wrapped his arms around her. "It would be a logical choice."

She stiffened again. He mentally cursed. It was so difficult to figure out her mood.

"Logic," she said. "You are right. It would be logical to marry you."

His heart soared. She agreed with him. He had not ruined his chances after all.

"I decline," she said.

His heart dropped into his stomach. "Why?"

OLIVIA'S FACE FELT hot, and tears burned in her eyes.

Logic.

A man who was dedicated to love, and he had chosen to woo her with the least romantic method available. She did not know why that mattered to her, but it did.

She could not help but wonder if he was hiding the true reason for his interest in her. The earl had wrapped her up in so many delusions that she'd given him everything. She was older and wiser, but the innocent girl still lived within her and had some sway over her actions. Was it Olivia or Lady Allen who was drawn to Thel? Did he truly love her, or did he simply wish for a woman to bear him an heir? If so, he would be disappointed to learn of the barren state of her womb.

No. Until she was certain of him, she could not risk anything more than a physical relationship. She searched for an excuse and clung to the first one she found.

"We still don't know why Mr. Dawson is after me, or how far he will go to ruin my reputation."

She turned, and the despondent look on his face almost undid her. She wanted to rush into his arms and promise him whatever he wanted. Her loyalty to him was already that strong. But that was what she would have done for the earl. Changed herself to suit his needs. She could not do that again.

"I don't care about your reputation," Thel said.

"I won't have people thinking I tricked you into marriage."

Thel ran a hand through his hair. "If that is what it takes." He gave her a lopsided grin. "You can be assured that when this matter is settled, I will ask again. At that time, I hope you will say 'yes.'"

She bit the inside of her cheek. The earl had never offered to do something for her unless it was clear she'd been expected to do something first to earn his devotion. She forced her emotions aside and focused on a matter that did not make her heart ache. "As for Constance, I believe the next event we should attend is Lord and Lady Wintermoor's masquerade tomorrow night."

He paused in the process of donning his trousers. "I have been to Lord and Lady Wintermoor's parties, Olivia. You will not find any acceptable suitors for Constance there."

"You cannot keep her locked up forever. The masquerade will give her something to focus on besides Mr. Dawson."

She would not tell him she had arranged for his daughter to sneak off with Mr. Dawson and test his resolve. The same part of her that urged her to test him insisted that if he was like her former husband, he would become angry at her for deceiving him.

It was foolish, given that Thel had displayed no signs of overwhelming affection or suffocating possession toward her, but it would not exit her mind. She would test him, as Constance was testing her unknown suitor. Once she was sure that he was not cut from the same cloth as the earl, then she would reveal everything.

Chapter Seventeen

JUSTICE DENIED. I cannot express my disappointment with Scotland Yard in strong enough terms. Despite being presented with ample evidence, they have allowed the murderous Lady Allen to remain a free woman. We must consider the possibility that she has lined the pockets of our local law enforcement officers. Perhaps it is time to take justice into our own hands.

N O ONE COULD deny Lord and Lady Wintermoor's masquerade was an absolute crush. Guests spilled out of the first-floor doors of the ballroom into the garden, and the sound of tittering laughter and even moans could be heard if one listened closely.

Olivia surveyed the mass of costumed revelers. Mr. Dawson was out there somewhere, if Constance was to be believed, and could spirit the girl away at any moment. She had only Constance's assurances that she would stay on the grounds and do nothing that might jeopardize her reputation.

She bumped into a man wearing a Roman toga and muttered her apologies. In other circumstances, the packed crowd would have made her anxious, but her costume was like a suit of armor, allowing her to take on a different role.

She touched the lacy edge of the bonnet atop her head. She had finally convinced Madame Julian to create the shepherdess costume gown from the dress plate she had seen in her shop. It had cost her several times more than what she would have paid for such a garment only a year prior, and she'd vexingly forgotten her shepherd's staff in her bedchamber, but she hoped Thel would approve.

Thel, who had asked her to be his wife. She'd spent the day avoiding him, using the excuse that she needed to prepare for the masquerade. She'd been trying to understand her own reservations. Thel was, on the surface, as far from the earl as it was possible to be. Yet some suspicious part of her refused to acknowledge he was genuine. She would not be his wife until she faced those fears. He deserved that much.

However, there was someone else she had to find before seeking Thel. The masquerade was the event of the season, which meant Mrs. Zephyr was sure to be lurking among the guests. Olivia did not know what costume the woman was wearing, but she felt confident she would recognize the woman's nasal voice even if she wore a sheet over her head.

She analyzed the colorful masks and costumes as she slipped through the crowd, making her own guesses as to the identity of each. The woman dressed as Cleopatra with a ruby-studded mask ordered the servants about and moved with a confidence reserved for the upper echelon of society. It could be none other than their hostess, the Duchess of Wintermoor, which meant the Mark Antony at her elbow was her husband.

Olivia veered away from the brightly dressed couple. Mrs. Zephyr was the kind of woman who preferred to gather her own crowd, rather than linger at the fringes of another. She also loved to hear herself speak, which meant she would not be near the orchestra.

The refreshment room, or the solarium. Which was more likely?

She chose the former, as it was closer, and picked her way through the crowd until she reached a long table covered in sweets. She picked up a chocolate-covered strawberry that had melted into goo from the heat. It was still delicious, tart, and

MENTOR TO THE MARQUESS

sweet in her mouth. She had been unable to eat that morning, as her stomach had twisted in knots at the thought of seeing Thel again.

She squared her shoulders. There was no point in delaying the inevitable. If she couldn't find her target, it was time to confront Thel and do her best to pretend nothing had happened. At least, until she'd made up her mind.

Suddenly, a heavy weight smashed into her and sent her sprawling.

"Oh, dear," a slurred voice said. "Who's that?"

Fate, it seemed, was on her side. Mrs. Zephyr's nasal voice was recognizable even in the woman's obviously drunk state.

She pushed upright, waving away the gloved hand that appeared in front of her, and faced Mrs. Zephyr. The woman was dressed in a green-and-blue peacock gown complete with long feathers that bobbed as she wavered on her feet. A mask lavishly appointed with sparkling, green stones obscured the top half of her face.

"I apologize for my rudeness," Mrs. Zephyr said. "I have consumed far too much champagne."

Olivia ensured her mask was still in place, then dropped into a deep curtsey usually reserved for women of much higher rank. The longer she could keep Mrs. Zephyr from recognizing her, the more likely she would be able to get the information she sought. "All is forgiven," Olivia said as she straightened. "I was hoping to speak to you, Mrs. Zephyr."

The woman flicked her head back, sending the peacock feathers fluttering. "You recognized me. Very clever. Well, wait no longer. How might I grace you with wisdom?"

"Were you familiar with the former Earl of Allen before he passed?"

Mrs. Zephyr clucked her tongue. "An impertinent question."

Olivia bowed her head, frantically forming a believable lie in her head. "I apologize, madam. It is only that my younger sister is considering becoming a companion to a lady who claims the previous earl left her a substantial fortune. I thought someone as important as you might know if there is any possibility the woman is telling the truth."

"Hmmm," Mrs. Zephyr said. She leaned in so close that her breath wreathed around Olivia's face. "I will impart a secret to you in exchange for bowling you over. I might have filled the role of the earl's mistress myself, except he had an understanding with a woman who was"—she put a shaking finger to her lips—"terribly jealous."

Shivers went up Olivia's arms. She put her hands on Mrs. Zephyr's shoulders to keep her from falling over. "Are you certain?"

"Do you call me a liar?" Mrs. Zephyr drew herself up. "She threatened me, you know. She said... What did she say? Ah, yes, she said the earl told her everything, including that I was a wet fish in bed." She huffed. "Envy is not a good look on a woman of her class."

Olivia leaned forward. "What was her name?"

She realized she had erred when Mrs. Zephyr scowled. "You're as jealous as that little, blonde whore." She staggered, nearly taking both of them off their feet. Olivia handed her off to a footman with instructions to take Mrs. Zephyr to a retiring room.

As the footman maneuvered his charge through the crowd, Olivia's mind buzzed with possibilities. Jealousy was a powerful motive, but it didn't explain why the articles had started years after her husband's death, or why Mr. Dawson had pursued Constance before Olivia had ever met the girl. Neither Mr. Dawson nor his unknown source could have possibly known that Thel would engage her as a matchmaker.

Or perhaps they could.

Every other matchmaker in London had rejected Thel, a wealthy marquess. Who had the power to make them do that?

As if summoned by her thoughts, Thel appeared by her side. He wore a black domino cloak, black trousers, and a black mask with two triangular ears.

"You look lovely," he said, kissing her white-gloved fingers.

The anxiety she'd expected to feel didn't come to her immense relief. She was also grateful he'd not called out her reluctance to see him. It made it easier to pretend things were normal between them.

"How did you know it was me?" she asked before his grin gave her the answer. "You bribed Mrs. Quill."

The maid had been remarkably helpful in procuring a length of light blue ribbon that Olivia had tied into bows and used to decorate her slippers.

He put a hand over his heart. "I would never."

She put her hand on his arm and let him draw her through the masses toward Constance, who wore a bright-yellow gown that sparkled in the gaslights. Her mask had wavy lines meant to represent the sun and was covered in gold leaf. Lily had balked at the expense, but Olivia had insisted. The bright costume acted as insurance. If the worst were to happen, Constance would be easy to recognize in the crowd.

"How are you enjoying the event?" she asked when they reached Constance.

The girl beamed. "It's wonderful!" She spun in a circle, spreading her skirt around her. "It is so freeing, being able to dress however I want without worrying about who will discuss it tomorrow."

"Stay in the ballroom," Thel said sharply. "The side rooms lead to..." He trailed off, then cleared his throat. "Activities not suitable for young ladies."

A young man appeared at Constance's side and linked his arm with hers. "Don't worry. I won't let her exclude me from her revels."

"Mr. Ringwell," Thel said, in a voice that conveyed no small amount of relief.

This was also Olivia's doing. With Constance's childhood friend present, it would be easier to convince Thel to let

Constance out of his sight. She was glad he had received her missive in time to prepare for the masquerade, and even more glad of his genuine interest in Constance. He was not a suitor she would have selected as a matchmaker, given his lack of title, but as long as Thel didn't disapprove, neither would she.

Constance twirled away from Mr. Ringwell. "Only if you can keep up with me." Then she darted into the crowd, a golden blur. Mr. Ringwell spared Olivia a nod before chasing after.

Thel tensed. Olivia saw it, attuned as she was to his movements.

"Are you certain it was wise to bring Constance here?" Thel asked. "Lord and Lady Wintermoor are not known for their discretion."

He was catching on. It would not be long before he realized the odds were good Mr. Dawson was present.

"I am perishing," she said. "Might we take a stroll outside?"

Thel looked between her and the quickly departing shape of Constance. "But…"

Constance had to have enough time to lose Mr. Ringwell, find Mr. Dawson, ask a question, and receive an answer that would make her seriously consider her future.

The crowd decided for them, jostling her and forcing the air from her lungs. She was nearly swept away from Thel, but with his height and size, he muscled through, grasping her hand and reeling her back like a fish on a line.

She pressed herself to his side until they were through the worst of the chaos. The tightness around her chest released, and she took a deep breath that wasn't scented with perfume. It was good that Saffron was not in attendance. She would surely have fled at the first sign of the crush.

Olivia tugged Thel's arm toward an outdoor stage. A group of actors was frozen in place in a *tableau vivant* depicting the daughter of Agamemnon being rescued from sacrifice by the goddess Diana. Each actor wore an elaborate mask that covered the entirety of their face.

She leaned closer and whispered into his ear, "I have a wicked idea."

He slid his hand down her back. "Oh?"

She nodded toward the stage. "We should join them."

Thel raised his eyebrows. "You want to try that?" He gestured to Iphigenia, splayed on a throne before them, wearing a gown so sheer, they could see the outlines of her nipples.

A thrill raced through Olivia. No one would know who they were. It was a perfect opportunity to distract Thel and experience something she'd always dreamed of but had never had the courage to pursue. The pursuit of pleasure in a public setting.

A chime sounded, and the actors shuffled off the stage, taking with them the throne and pillows.

She tugged him up, and they approached a door beneath the stage. They stepped into a dark room filled with trunks.

"Perfect," she whispered.

"What exactly do you expect to happen?" Thel asked, closing the door behind them. "They are hardly likely to allow guests to trot onto the stage."

She pried open the lid of a trunk and found exactly what she was looking for, as if fate had placed it in her path. "They will if they don't know who we are."

"You cannot be serious."

She was already removing her mask and the many layers of her costume. When she was down to her undergarments, she pulled a plain gown of spun wool out of the trunk and slipped it over her head. She had seen some actors wearing similar outfits in the crowd when they were not performing on stage. With luck, they would fit right in.

She turned to Thel with a flourish.

"A remarkable transformation," Thel said dryly. "I can hardly tell you spent several hours with a maid this evening."

She brought her hands to her hair. "Oh. I had forgotten."

Thel chuckled. "Allow me."

He walked behind her and dug his fingers into her hair, removing the sharp pins until her locks tumbled free.

He pressed a kiss to the back of her spine. "The jewelry as well?"

"Y-Yes, of course."

He traced the curve of her ear with his finger. "At this rate, we will not make it to the stage."

As tempting as that offer was, a part of her wanted to experience the attention of the crowd upon her, appreciating her body without knowing they were salivating over a woman they had scorned.

She stepped out of Thel's embrace and purloined a pair of trousers and a shirt for him. When he had changed, she balled up her clothing and held it in her arms. Where could they store their garments such that no one would stumble upon them?

"Let me." Thel peeked out the door and summoned a footman with a crook of his finger. One whispered conversation and exchange of coins later, and the footman took off with the evidence of their identities.

She took his hand and pulled him up the stairs, where another door waited.

Any fears that they would not fit in were swept aside as the other actors took one look at them, chastised them for being late, and hustled them into separate dressing areas.

Olivia allowed a young woman to pull her purloined gown off and tried not to giggle as a new one was thrust over her head. Her hair was tucked beneath a wig, and a mask was lowered over her face.

She was shoved next to a mirror and looked at herself in wonder. The gown was something her grandmother might have worn, sleek and with a square neckline and no more substantial than a night rail. The mask covered her from forehead to chin and was feathered and dusted with silver jewels and tendrils of blonde hair that curled around her cheeks.

She swallowed past a lump in her throat. She could not believe what she was about to do. Strangers would see her in such a revealing outfit. She should walk away, find some other way of distracting Thel while Constance was speaking to Mr. Dawson.

A short, curvy woman wearing a sprig of laurels atop her curly, brown head crouched at Olivia's feet and plucked strands of grass from her gown. When she'd finished, she stood and put her hands on her hips. "Does it suffice, my lady?"

The formal manner of address made her stiffen.

The woman winked. "Don't worry. We've no concern about you and your... friend taking a turn. Gives us more time to prepare for the next one."

"Ah, then, yes." Olivia nodded. "It is lovely. Thank you. Ah... what role will I be playing?"

"The Loves of Acis and Galatea."

Olivia knew it. Alexandre Charles Guillemot's work told of the love between the mortal Acis and the sea-nymph Galatea. She plucked the sheer fabric of her costume. "Aren't I wearing too much?" In the painting, Galatea wore nothing but a sheet around her waist.

The woman did not answer, but bustled her out of the dressing area and then Olivia was on the stage. For several seconds, she froze. Then a murmur rippled through the crowd, and Olivia remembered what she was supposed to be doing. She strolled across the stage, head high, and reached a bundle of silver fabric pooled in front of a box covered in a red sheet. She splayed down on the ground, assuming her role. The moment she froze in place, another actor stepped onto the stage from the other side. She could not see his face beneath the elaborate mask covered in blue and green flowers, but he was clothed in brown sandals and a matching Roman toga that barely covered his thick carpet of chest hair.

It was Thel, wearing less than she was.

He sat on the rock behind her. Taking his cue, she placed her arm across his lap and tilted her head to the sky. Their garb did not exactly match the painting they were emulating, but it was enough for the audience to erupt in applause.

Her insides twisted and her cheeks felt warm. Seconds passed like minutes as she held herself as still as possible. She dared not move or touch him, as she feared her confidence would shatter and she would flee the stage.

"Look at me," he whispered.

She met his gaze, and the intensity in his eyes made her want to reach up and kiss him. His expression was hidden beneath his mask, but the muscles in his shoulders and neck were taut, as if he were holding himself back.

The music changed, indicating it was time to adjust positions. A wicked impulse had her throwing away her prior concerns and crawling on Thel's lap, straddling him with her arms around his neck. He clasped his hands about her waist and squeezed, making her gasp. Rather than ruin the illusion, she leaned back until her head was tilted to the sky. They froze in that position, although at least one part of him continued to move, or more accurately, *grow*.

"I don't know how much more I can take of this," he whispered in a pained voice.

She chewed the inside of her cheek to keep from laughing. In a sense, his costume was even more revealing than hers. "Carry me off when the song ends."

He grumbled but remained in position until the music faded. Then she wrapped her legs around his hips and twisted her torso to wave at the cheering crowd as Thel carried her offstage.

Chapter Eighteen

"I T'S CAUGHT ON my corset," Olivia said from beneath her dress. Thel lifted the fabric, but the damned dress was so light, it fluttered in the slight breeze coming from the open window and tangled further. Olivia struggled until the sheer fabric was draped over her bodice and head until she resembled a ghost. He tickled her sides, making her break into laughter. She bumped a rack of cue sticks on the wall and sent them clattering to the ground. Before she could trip over them, he pushed her into a chair and placed the items back in their places beside the billiards table.

The other actors had left them alone in what appeared to be a gaming room with a raised eyebrow and a wink, as if they knew what they wanted to do. Another whispered word to a footman and their costumes were delivered shortly after. He had already donned his, but Olivia was having more difficulty.

She struggled out of his grip and brutally yanked the fabric off. She tossed it at her feet, then made an exaggerated gasping sound as if she had just come up from beneath the water.

"I thought I would never escape," she said.

Thel leaned back and took in the shape of her waist in the corset and drawers. "I could have stood to see you struggle a bit more."

His skin was still dewy from the performance. He could not believe they had done it. The way Olivia had reclined on the stage had made his insides twist. She was so daring, a wild woman he wanted by his side. If only she would agree to be his wife.

She stuck out her tongue, then plucked strands of silk tulle that clung to the metal clasps of her corset, drooping down like strands of spider silk.

"I have a present for you," she said.

"Oh?" he asked.

She touched her bodice. "You must unwrap it."

He reached for her waist, sliding his hands up before unclasping her corset until it came free. Then he dropped to his knees and smoothed his palms along her stockinged shins. He drew her chemise up until it gathered at her waist. She tore it off and stood bare from the waist up.

His mouth went dry. She had threaded rings through her pierced nipples and attached a chain that lay between her breasts like an undulating snake.

His cock throbbed. The glinting silver metal on her soft skin was almost more than he could take.

She took his hand and laid it on top of the chain. "Tug ever so slightly."

He did so, and she obligingly stepped forward, drawn by the pressure on her bosom.

He dipped his head and took a ring-clad nipple into his mouth. The metallic bite on his tongue was foreign, but not unpleasant, and her skin smelled of soap and roses. He slid his hands up her back, pressing her into him as she made soft, breathy noises.

"Remove them," she whispered.

He took a ring in his teeth and fumbled with the clasp until it clicked open. She hissed as it left her flesh. He touched his lips to her nipple and ran the tip of his tongue along the hole that remained.

"The other one," she said.

He repeated the procedure on her other nipple before depositing the chain and rings in his pocket. Then he captured her mouth.

Her hands quickly undid the buttons on his jacket, and then his shirt, and spread the fabric wide. Her fingers curled into his chest hair. He loved it when she did that and loved even more the feel of her nails running along his skin.

He lifted her by the waist and carried her to the chaise, then juggled her in his arms until she was curled against his chest, his erection pressed into her bottom.

He kept his hands on her waist as she freed his cock and groaned when she rubbed the entire length of him in her essence. She positioned him against her entrance and caught his lips in a kiss while sliding down his length in one long, languid movement, until she was seated fully. He was so aroused from their activities and watching her undress that he nearly spent himself in that moment.

Then she pressed her lips to his, squeezed herself around him, and he was lost.

He threw his head back as an orgasm rocked through him. "My God, woman, you will be the death of me."

"There is much still to learn," she said as she lifted herself off his lap. She turned her head around the room before stopping her gaze at his neckcloth.

He splayed his hand over his throat. "Absolutely not." He reached into his jacket and removed a folded square of fabric. A handkerchief. She accepted it and gently cleaned the result of their exertions away.

Before he realized what she was doing, she had gently tied one of her garter ribbons into a bow around the base of his shaft.

"What is this?" he asked, amused. "It is a remarkable specimen, but a gift?"

"It will be our secret," Olivia said. "Send me the chains when you wish me to wear them and wear my token in return."

His body flushed with heat and as she slipped her chemise back on, the ribbon chafed. He adjusted himself, and she shot him a sultry look.

His cock twitched again. She knew what the ribbon was doing to him.

He wanted to bend her over right there and take her again. He stuck his hand into his pocket and let the chain run through his fingers. It would be a challenge not to send it to her immediately, but he preferred to draw out their pleasure through anticipation.

He removed the ribbon, warm from the heat of his body, and folded it into his pocket with the chain.

If he were to do as she bid, it would have to be at a ball where he was not expected to dance. Knowing what she was wearing beneath her gown would be too much of a distraction for him to take any other woman into his arms.

WHEN THEL RETURNED to the ballroom with Olivia on his arm, it was to find Constance in the refreshment room on the arm of a black-haired man wearing a star-studded cape and a crescent moon mask. He leaned close to Constance and whispered something in her ear that made her erupt into giggles and bump into the table, spilling lemonade onto the floor.

The night had barely begun, and his daughter was already drunk.

"Who is that man?" Olivia asked.

"Not Mr. Ringwell," he said. "Where the hell did that boy get off to?"

He had trusted Mr. Ringwell to stay by Constance's side. He would not have left them alone if he had suspected the boy had not been committed to his task.

Constance spotted them and clutched the arm of her companion. "F-Father. I was looking for you. This is—"

"Allow me," the unknown man interrupted. He swished his

cape and bowed. "John Dawson."

The chatter of the surrounding crowd shushed to a dull hum threaded through with a high-pitched whine. So, this was the man who had crept into his daughter's life and disrupted his plans for her future.

"It is a pleasure to meet you," Olivia said tightly.

"Indeed." A muscle in Mr. Dawson's cheek pulsed. "I am surprised to see you here, Lady Allen, given what is being said about you."

She clenched Thel's arm. "I was never one to let rumors spoil my fun. We have arranged to attend several events in the coming days to ensure Constance is properly introduced to society."

"Ah, but..." Dawson flicked his gaze to Constance, then to Thel, then back to Olivia. "Constance does not require introductions."

The unsaid words *if we are to marry* hung between them like dust floating in the air, visible but unremarked upon. Thel imagined planting his fist into Dawson's face. He would wrap his hands around the man's neck until the smug smile vanished from his face.

"Perhaps you might advise me, Mr. Dawson," Olivia said loudly. "Constance mentioned you are to inherit your father's rail company. As it happens, I am looking to invest."

The change in subject gave Thel enough time to recover himself, and in doing so, he realized why Olivia had stepped in.

Confidence radiated off Dawson in waves. He was not perturbed by the less-than-gracious reception.

Then it hit him. It was as Olivia had warned. If he disapproved overtly, Dawson would become the victim and elicit sympathy from Constance.

He had almost played into Dawson's hands.

Thankfully, Dawson wasn't looking so confident anymore. He frowned at Olivia. "I would not think it appropriate for a lady to engage in business matters."

She waved her hand. "Where I choose to invest is of no concern to society." She leaned forward. "I have significant funds I could dispense, given the right opportunity."

Dawson's eyes widened. "Indeed?"

That one small interaction told Thel everything he needed to know about Dawson's relationship with money. This was not a man who was accustomed to wealth.

"Oh, Lady Allen!" Constance said. "John has agreed to wait until I am one-and-twenty to marry. Isn't that wonderful?"

"How lovely," Olivia said in a strangled voice.

Thel's explosive response was stifled by Olivia stomping his foot. He tucked his hands behind his back and balled them into fists. Everything was happening too quickly. Constance had only attended half a dozen events, but she had already chosen her husband.

"'Lovely' is not precisely the word I would use," he said.

Dawson leaned forward. "Do you disapprove, my lord? Your daughter and I are in love. Marriage is the natural consequence."

Constance grinned. "Isn't it wonderful, Father? I have found my true love."

The sharp edges of the trap closed tightly around Thel's heart. Everything Olivia had predicted was coming true. Constance clung to her inappropriate suitor tighter than a shipwreck survivor around a chunk of flotsam. The moment he made his displeasure known, he would lose her.

Dawson had won.

"I only meant that 'lovely' is not strong enough to express my delight," Thel said, forcing the words out. "This is marvelous news. A spectacular turn of events."

Dawson's smile faltered. "Ah, yes, well." He tugged at his collar then continued in a louder voice. "I must applaud your bravery, my lord. Few men would be comfortable associating with a woman who has such a"—he shot Olivia a triumphant look—"sordid past."

The sudden change in tone and topic made Olivia's jaw drop, but Thel was not similarly affected.

"Being a widow is not in the least scandalous," Thel said. "Mr. Dawson, you must learn these things if you are to blend in with the *ton*."

The thunderous look on Dawson's face nearly undid him.

Olivia flicked open her fan and used it to hide what was visible of her face behind her mask.

"A widow, perhaps," Dawson said scathingly. "But only because he died before she could petition for divorce."

Olivia gasped and clutched Thel's arm. "How did—how dare you!"

"Let us not forget that these accusations are mere gossip," Thel said loudly. "No proof has been levied against Lady Allen."

Dawson inclined his head. "Of course. I apologize for my outburst. I am only concerned about the welfare of your daughter. I would not want any improper rumors to become attached to her."

Thel's rude response was lost in the opening notes of the orchestra. He clenched his hands and stepped forward, but Olivia held him back.

"Why are you doing this?" she asked Dawson.

"My dear Lady Allen." He leaned in and whispered in her ear, "I'm giving you exactly what you deserve." Then he swept Constance into his arms and merged into the flow of dancers.

Chapter Nineteen

"*I*'M GIVING YOU *exactly what you deserve.*"

Mr. Dawson's ominous comment echoed in Olivia's mind. Even though she had never met him, he knew that before the earl's death, she had been gathering evidence to petition for divorce under the Matrimonial Causes Act, something she had kept a closely guarded secret. The only person who had known was the earl… and anyone he had told.

That was proof enough for her that Mr. Dawson was in league with the late Earl of Allen's mistress.

The only thing left to find out was the identity of said lady. They could not threaten Mr. Dawson without risking Constance, but perhaps the woman could be reasoned with, or persuaded in some other way.

Unfortunately, she had few clues, beyond the woman being blonde, married, and a member of the gentry. Mrs. Zephyr was unlikely to remember their conversation in the morning, much less be willing to elaborate.

There had to be someone else who had seen her husband's mistress enter her home. A carriage driver. A street sweeper. Perhaps if she brought sketches of different women to Boris, it would jog his memory.

Thel shook her shoulders, scrambling her thoughts. She was no longer standing in the ballroom but sitting in an armchair in a candlelit office with Thel gazing at her face.

"Tell me what to do," he said.

She should have confessed everything: that she had arranged for Constance to sneak away with Mr. Dawson and test him, that her plan had failed, and now Constance was betrothed. Worse, Olivia had no idea what Mr. Dawson was planning. He couldn't intend to keep Constance unaware of his lies for three more years.

Thel cupped her cheek in his hand. "You can trust me."

She leaned into his touch and forced her stiff muscles to relax even as fear of what he might do if she angered him caused her words to curdle in her throat.

"That's better," Thel said. "I thought you might faint, and I wasn't keen on carrying your unconscious body back to the carriage."

She imagined him being caught by a laundry maid while prowling through the hallways with her limp form draped across his shoulder like a barbarian and giggled.

He pressed his forehead to hers. "Laughter suits you."

She indulged him for a long moment before pulling away. As Mr. Dawson had passed Constance's test—although she doubted he had meant anything he had told the young girl—so had Thel passed hers. She owed him the truth.

"Mr. Dawson is here because of me," she said before filling him in on what she had instructed Constance to do. "I took a chance. If it had worked, we might have been free of him." She clenched her back teeth together. "Now she is more confident in him than ever."

He knelt in front of her and put his hand on her thigh. "Why didn't you tell me?"

She turned her head away. "I didn't think you would approve."

He shoved to his feet. "Of course I don't approve!"

She wanted to throw herself into his arms and beg for his forgiveness, but that would do nothing to resolve the problem they faced.

She pulled her knees to her chest and wrapped her arms around them. "There's more." She told him about her brief conversation with Mrs. Zephyr and her subsequent suspicions.

"A blonde, married woman." Thel exhaled harshly through his nostrils. "It could be one of a hundred different ladies. How do we narrow it down?"

"I will consult *Debrett's Peerage*," she said. "That is, at least, a place to start." Even if it meant many long nights at her desk trying to summon a mental image of each name in the book.

"I could speak to Mrs. Zephyr," he said.

She shook her head. "She would not tell you anything that sensitive without first securing an invitation to your bed." The woman was too conniving, and she'd already made her interest in Thel clear.

He shuddered. "In that case, I'll leave her to you."

"That still leaves Mr. Dawson," she said. He was the more immediate threat, having sauntered into her trap without triggering the snare. That meant he would likely see through any obvious attempt she made at manipulation.

The connection between her former husband's jealous mistress and Mr. Dawson still eluded her. She had searched the earl's paperwork, but there was no mention of him. She didn't know if he was the puppet master or a pawn in another woman's game. His actions had not endeared her to him, but she had to consider the possibility that she had only focused on him because her past colored any man like the earl as a monster.

Then she remembered the bruises on Lady Mason's arm and realized the only thing that mattered was removing Constance from Mr. Dawson's reach. The longer she remained attached to him, the more likely she would wind up dead or chained to a man who treated her as a possession.

She forced her thoughts back on track. "He has power over us as long as he continues commissioning the articles and has his hooks in Constance."

Although, the more she considered Constance's behavior, the

more she wondered if Constance knew anything about what Mr. Dawson was doing. Had he somehow arranged the articles without her knowing? What of the letters found in Constance's room? The girl *had* seemed ignorant of them.

Thel scowled. "If I challenged him to a duel, it would be by morning."

She shook her head. "You do not have sufficient reason to call him out. Even if you did, and assuming you were even the victor, her grief would eventually fade, but she would never forgive you. If we are to have any chance of beating Mr. Dawson, it must be in the place where we have the most influence and control. Within society." She sighed. "She trusts me. If we give her enough time, she'll come to her senses. The difficulty will be in keeping Mr. Dawson from realizing what we are doing."

She had some idea of what might entice him. Her former husband had loved nothing more than drawing out her suffering. It was only when she'd failed to give him a reaction that he'd grown impatient and things had escalated. If Mr. Dawson was the same, then for Constance's sake, she would put on the most elaborate performance of her life.

"Let me help," a voice said.

Mr. Ringwell stood in the doorway, dressed in a different suit than he had worn earlier that evening. His hair was wet, and there was a damp towel clutched in his hand.

"What happened to you?" Thel asked.

Mr. Ringwell's lips thinned. "When I wouldn't let Constance wander off without me, she pushed me into a fountain. Lord Wintermoor found me and allowed me to borrow one of his suits." He lifted his arm. The cuff of his jacket dangled over the tips of his fingers. "We are not quite of the same size."

Olivia put a knuckle to her lips but could not completely disguise her laugh. He looked like a child who had been playing in his father's wardrobe. Constance would owe him a significant apology if she had any interest in maintaining their friendship.

Mr. Ringwell rubbed his hair with his towel. "She told me

about Mr. Dawson. It's not the first time I've seen her besotted. She'll come out of it." He squeezed the towel so tight that the tips of his fingers turned white. "She has to."

"I wish I had known there was something between you two," Thel said. "It might have saved me the trouble of finding a matchmaker." Then he cursed as Mr. Ringwell shook his wet hair, spraying droplets of water.

Olivia stood and paced the room. When she compared the situation to her own coming out, Mr. Ringwell was the most significant difference. Her childhood had been devoid of friends. Every young man she had met at her first ball had been a stranger. The earl had used her lack of experience to his advantage, placing himself above her other suitors by virtue of his greater fortune and title.

"Mr. Ringwell can assist us by preventing Mr. Dawson from capturing the entirety of Constance's attention," she said. "Mr. Dawson will find it difficult to control her while there is someone else whispering in her ear, and because she treats him like a friend, Mr. Dawson might not see him as a threat."

Mr. Ringwell winced. "You do not need to remind me."

"Do not start," Thel said. "If you had expressed your feelings to her sooner, she might never have fallen in with Mr. Dawson to begin with."

Mr. Ringwell's ears turned red. "I know. It's only that when it comes to Constance, the practiced speeches vanish from my mind the moment we're alone. I had all but given up on her until you left for London. It was only then that I realized that I couldn't let her marry someone else." He shuffled his feet. "I tried to confess tonight, but my tongue twisted into knots and the words wouldn't come out."

"I'm sorry," Olivia said. She knew exactly how it felt to be overwhelmed with emotion to the point where she couldn't speak.

"I did ask her to marry me once," Mr. Ringwell said. "When we were children. I even gave her a ring made of braided grass."

MENTOR TO THE MARQUESS

He touched his breast pocket, where Olivia suspected another such ring was stored.

"You will have another chance," Thel said. Then he looked at Olivia. "How shall we start our campaign?"

She would never grow tired of the way he deferred to her, especially when they both knew she was the expert in a given area.

"I'll tell Constance the only way she can convince her family to accept Mr. Dawson is by showing them he can exist in society alongside her," she said. "That way, we can control how and when they meet."

"And she won't get away from me again," Mr. Ringwell said. "Even if it means I drag her into the fountain with me next time."

Chapter Twenty

MURDERESS INTENDED DIVORCE. It is with great pleasure I can reveal, at last, Lady Allen's motive for the heinous murder of her husband, the Earl of Allen. The earl, having grown suspicious of his wife, discovered a cache of paperwork that suggested she intended to petition for divorce. Enraged by her disloyalty, the earl confronted his wife and informed her he would oppose the petition. In doing so, he sealed his fate.

I T HAD BEEN years since Thel had regularly ridden a horse, but the steady *clip-clop* of horse hooves on the path and the wind rustling the leaves drew him back to his youth and the afternoons spent hunched over the neck of his chubby, gray pony, determined to impress his father.

Unfortunately, his daughter's excitement meant he could not fully enjoy the moment.

"A spring wedding would be best, but winter is so beautiful," she said. "I wish I could tell everyone. Are you certain I must wait? John was not happy when I insisted on secrecy."

He had gone over this point enough that he was comfortable answering. "They need time to adjust to the idea of you being courted at all, my dear. It will be years until you marry. We will tell them about your betrothal when the time is right."

That was also the reason they were awake far earlier than usual, while the rest of his family lay abed.

Constance huffed. "I suppose. Do you think grandmother would lend me her pearls? I'll need a sprig of myrtle for my bouquet, of course, and carnations to symbolize faithfulness…"

He only realized his daughter's brown and white-spotted mare was straying off the path when her voice grew quieter.

He pulled his horse up short. "Constance, keep next to me."

She returned to the path, but in less than a minute, her mount was wandering away again.

"Constance," he said.

"Give her a moment; the poor dear is hungry." She patted her horse's neck as the animal delicately plucked dandelions from the grass.

Olivia trotted her mount up next to him. "Have you seen Mr. Ringwell?"

"No, but the day is yet young," he said.

Mr. Ringwell was meant to meet them during their second rotation of the park, which they had nearly completed. Thel's idea was to show Constance that Mr. Ringwell was more than a silly village boy by displaying his more positive traits. As the boy was skilled with horses, and the park was a neutral enough ground, they started with riding.

"No Mr. Dawson, either," Olivia said.

"He'll come," Thel said, speaking with more confidence than he felt. Dawson's presence was another part of their plan. Thel presumed that having come from America, he would not be as confident on horseback and would serve as a contrast to Mr. Ringwell's skill.

"I grow weary of playing the downtrodden lady already," Olivia said. She stuck a finger between the high, black collar and her neck. "I did not expect to wear my widow's weeds again so soon, but I needed them to settle into the role of the overwhelmed, downtrodden woman I must play to keep Mr. Dawson unaware of our plans. I wasn't sure it would work until I closed the top button of my collar. It was like I was thrust back to those first few weeks after the funeral when I kept expecting the earl to rise from his grave and haunt me."

Thel adjusted a black ostrich feather in her hat that had fallen forward. "It is not too late for me to get my dueling pistols out of storage."

"Absolutely not." She grasped the bottom of her bodice and tugged it down. "I will think of it as playing the role of myself from the darkest years of my marriage, with Mr. Dawson as the earl."

Thel gave an exaggerated shudder. "Please do not speak of such things."

Olivia's giggles were interrupted by the sound of rapidly approaching hoofbeats. Thel turned in time to see Constance shift from cooing over her horse to gaping at the transformed Mr. Ringwell.

Thel could hardly recognize the boy. He was dressed as regally as a duke in a tan tailcoat with notched lapels. The high collar of his snowy-white shirt was held in place by a dark-green cravat, and his black leather riding boots gleamed.

"Good morning, Lady Constance," he said. His horse dipped its head and drew one leg back in a rather spectacular bow.

Constance stared at Mr. Ringwell for so long that Thel wondered if she had even heard the boy speak.

"Connie," Mr. Ringwell said softly.

She snapped her jaw shut and flicked her reins, but her mare refused to budge.

Mr. Ringwell rode next to her mare and peered at her saddle. "Looks like she sucked in air. Shall I fix it?"

"That would be most convenient, Mr. Ringwell."

As Mr. Ringwell dismounted, Thel leaned closer to Olivia and whispered, "I think it's working."

Samuel Ringwell had not been "Mr. Ringwell" to his daughter for as long as he could remember. He hoped her referring to him in a more formal manner suggested she was seeing him as more than a childhood friend.

When Mr. Ringwell finished cinching Constance's saddle,

they continued along the loop.

It was comfortable riding beside Olivia while watching over his daughter. It almost felt as if she were his wife. If they had not been waiting for Dawson to swoop in and disrupt the moment, he might have suggested they find a chaperone for Constance and sneak off to enjoy themselves.

"I wish we were somewhere more private," Olivia said. She licked her bottom lip. "Perhaps when this is over, you might pay me a visit. I have several fascinating implements I believe you would quite enjoy."

He remembered the glint of metal on her breasts, and his trousers were suddenly too tight. He had learned more about intimate acts from her in a few short days than he had ever gleaned from his dusty texts.

He sidled his horse closer. "It would be my pleasure."

She squeezed his thigh. "My dear, there would be enough pleasure for both of us."

Despite his better nature, he was about to suggest they ride back to his house when a fast-moving dark splotch across the park drew his attention. He took Olivia's hand and squeezed it. "Tonight. For now, we must resume our roles."

She straightened. "Mr. Dawson?"

He did not have a chance to answer, as in the next moment, the man in question trotted toward them on a dark bay stallion. Without the crescent moon mask, Thel got a different impression of the man. Dawson was older than he had realized, nearly Olivia's age, and the cut of his suit was inferior, especially compared to Mr. Ringwell's. However, he handled his mount with the same level of skill and confidence as his rival.

"Lady Allen," Dawson said, with a slight incline of his head. "I am impressed with your resolve. There are few women who would dare venture out with such grave accusations levied against them."

"The rumors will pass," Olivia said. There was a slight tremor in her voice, and she stared directly ahead with an expression so still, it reminded Thel of a porcelain doll.

"Such confidence."

She curled her shoulders inward. "My affairs are none of your concern."

Thel flexed his hands, stiff from clutching the reins. He did not dare speak up for fear of disrupting Olivia's act. Part of their plan involved keeping Dawson feeling as if he were in control. If Thel made his displeasure known, Dawson might realize they were aware of his scheme. Thus, he held his silence.

Dawson lifted his chin and moved his horse ahead.

Olivia joined him as he increased speed. He was willing to grant Mr. Ringwell the privilege of speaking with Constance in private, but not Dawson.

"There must be another young lady in this park who would enjoy your company, Mr. Ringwell," Dawson said. "There are matters I wish to discuss with my betrothed in private."

The hair on the back of Thel's neck rose, but he held his tongue. If Mr. Ringwell was going to have any success in bringing Constance to her senses, he needed to do it without her father interfering.

As it turned out, Mr. Ringwell did not need to respond.

"We will have plenty of time to discuss the wedding before I turn one-and-twenty," Constance said. "Mr. Ringwell, when was the last time you visited the village? I find I am missing home."

"I was there a fortnight ago and will be returning soon to inspect our horses before the derby." He patted his stallion's neck. "Murphy was a prize winner, back in my father's day."

"Rather fond of the derby myself," Dawson said loudly.

A change came over Mr. Ringwell then, one Thel recognized from the many times the boy's father had forbidden him from driving the carriage, or swimming across the gushing river, or climbing behind the wool pile. As such, Mr. Ringwell's next words were no surprise.

"Fancy a wager, Mr. Dawson?"

An hour later, Thel found himself amid a crowd of curious

ladies and gentlemen. A section of the path had been cleared and lines drawn in chalk about a hundred yards apart. To carry out this task, Mr. Ringwell and Dawson had engaged a dozen riders to wait along the edges of the track at equal distances to keep anyone from accidentally straying too close. Several of said gentlemen had already made discreet wagers, and from what he could gather, Mr. Ringwell was the favorite.

A shot rang out, and the riders were off like a blur, spraying gravel in their wake. The crowd erupted into cheers.

"Go, Mr. Ringwell!" Constance yelled.

The horses remained within inches of each other as they approached the end of the path. The next section was the most difficult, as it required them to slow down enough to make a complete turn before returning the way they had come. Mr. Ringwell completed the task gracefully, hardly even cutting into the grass. Dawson followed close behind but was steadily losing ground.

A cloud of dust kicked up by galloping hooves made it diffi-cult to see. It also started a chorus of coughing and sneezing. Thel held a handkerchief to his nose with one hand and grabbed his saddle horn with the other.

Constance's horse shifted and rolled her eyes. If they were not flanked by other riders, he suspected the animal would have bolted.

"They've rounded the turn," Olivia said.

He barely heard her over the increasing volume of cheers.

In the few seconds it took for both riders to pass them, Mr. Ringwell earned a slight lead.

"Come on, Mr. Ringwell!" he yelled, even as the dust became so thick, he could barely see. He peered closer and caught a flash of silver from Dawson. There was a faint whinny, and then Mr. Ringwell fell back, just in time for Dawson to thunder across the finish line. He was immediately mobbed by a deafening wave of well-wishers.

As the dust settled, he turned, only to find his daughter's

saddle empty.

He searched the surrounding area but did not see her. "Constance!"

The riotous noise of celebration dimmed to a shush, and the enormous crowd seemed to expand until he could see nothing else. There were so many people. Any sudden sound could spark a stampede, and his daughter might be trampled.

A second voice joined him, shouting Constance's name as Olivia shoved closer. Some of the excited winners had realized the danger of the situation and were urging people to back away.

He spun his horse around, his heart in his throat, until at last, he spotted Constance lingering near the finish line next to Mr. Ringwell.

A sense of lightness passed over him so quickly that he was momentarily dizzy.

"That was too close for my comfort," Olivia said. "I am not sure how she even dismounted on her own." She tugged Constance's horse forward. The mare stopped the moment Olivia gave her slack and then dropped her head to the ground, nostrils flaring.

"Stubborn beast," she said. "Shall we reunite them?"

Constance laughed at something Mr. Ringwell had said, completely unaware of the chaos she had caused by disappearing.

"Not that I am complaining," Thel said. "But shouldn't she be congratulating the winner?"

Olivia clucked her tongue. "You have much to learn about women, my lord."

As they approached, a horse in the middle of the chaos bucked, starting a chain reaction that rippled through the crowd. Thel stayed astride, but Olivia had to drop the reins to Constance's horse to avoid falling, and in the process, the horse bucked free and charged toward Constance.

He shouted his daughter's name, but she remained frozen, like a deer staring down the barrel of a musket.

He was too far away to reach her in time. Unless the horse

veered away, she would be trampled. The scenario unfolded in his mind. He would race toward her, scramble from his horse, and bundle her body in his arms. She would slip through his fingers the same way Marguerite had, and he would be alone again.

Then Mr. Ringwell tackled Constance, and they rolled out of the path of the stampeding animal.

Thel dismounted with such haste that he nearly got caught in his stirrup. He shook his foot free and stumbled across the grass, his heart thundering, then fell to his knees beside his daughter.

Mr. Ringwell clutched Constance to his chest as she stared, unseeing, over his shoulder.

"That was too close," Olivia said from behind him.

Thel cupped his daughter's cheek. "Are you okay?"

"Father?" She pulled away from Mr. Ringwell and looked around. "Where's John?"

He wanted to hug her and strangle her at the same time. "You nearly got yourself killed, and that's all you say? It wasn't Mr. Dawson who saved you."

Her eyes filled with tears. "He didn't? He didn't even try?" Then she tucked her head into Mr. Ringwell's shoulder with a sob.

"This is my fault," Mr. Ringwell said, his face grave. He met Thel's gaze squarely. "I should not have challenged Mr. Dawson."

That Mr. Ringwell was right did not blunt the bone-deep feeling that Thel had failed to protect his daughter. She'd barely been able to control her horse, and the animal had shown signs of bolting at the beginning of the race, but he'd pushed his concerns away in the hope that watching Mr. Ringwell win would tip Constance's favor in his direction.

"She's had a shock," Olivia said as she crouched beside him. "We should return her to her room before we attract any more attention."

He reluctantly rose to his feet and allowed Mr. Ringwell to guide Constance back to her horse. She refused to mount but accepted the mare's reins and walked alongside her. Then the sound of a horse galloping had them all turning to see Dawson racing toward them.

"Constance!" Dawson cried. He pulled up his horse, hastily dismounted, then ran toward them, alarm written across his features.

"I've got her," Mr. Ringwell said, holding out a hand as if to ward Dawson off.

"Nonsense," Dawson said. He shoved past Mr. Ringwell and reached for Constance, but she flinched.

Dawson dropped his arms and frowned. "What's wrong?"

"I-I have to go home," Constance said. She stepped closer to Mr. Ringwell, who crossed his arms and pressed his lips into a thin line. Thel suspected it would not take much for Mr. Ringwell to escalate to violence.

"But…" Dawson looked at Mr. Ringwell, seemed to freeze in place for a moment, then shook his head. "Fine. Do as you wish." He spun on his heel and walked back to his mount without a single glance back.

Chapter Twenty-One

AUTHORITIES DRAW CLOSE. Additional evidence of Lady Allen's misdeeds has been provided to the members of London's finest. It shall not be long before Lady Allen receives the justice she richly deserves.

I F SOMEONE HAD asked Olivia how many blonde, married women of high class there were in society, she might have shrugged and guessed about fifty.

She would have been wrong.

The real number was at least twice that, and she had only counted those who lived in or regularly visited London.

She slammed her copy of *Debrett's* closed. Hours of carefully combing through the earl's correspondence and she was no closer to uncovering the identity of her former husband's mistress.

There had to be a faster way. She had commissioned one of Saffron's artist friends to produce sketches of the most likely suspects, but Boris's eyesight was not good enough for him to say if any of them had been the woman he had seen.

She wished they could have revealed Mr. Dawson's trickery in full to the rest of Thel's family, but it was too risky. They did not know how Thel's parents or brothers would react and the last thing they needed was a fistfight in the middle of the parlor.

Maybe Thel had been right all along, and the best way to get rid of Mr. Dawson was to put a bullet through his heart. It would solve both of their problems at the same time. Then again, after the stunt in the park, she'd caught more than a few glances of Constable Smith out of the corner of her eye. The man was watching her, perhaps waiting for an opportunity to question her again. If she gave him a chance to arrest either Thel or herself, he might pounce.

A knock at her door gave her the perfect excuse to take a break. "Come in."

Her butler entered, clutching a wax-sealed envelope and a small box. "From Lord Lowell, my lady." He set the items at the edge of her desk. "The cook insisted on feeding the messenger, seeing as it is nearly teatime. Shall I instruct him to wait?"

Olivia's arms burst into gooseflesh. She did not need to see inside the box to know what it held. She had wondered how long Thel would wait before returning her chain. She imagined him tying her silk garter around himself, preparing her present. Their pleasure would be that much more intense from the waiting.

Her butler was still waiting for her response.

"Send the boy back with a basket of apple tarts from this morning," she said. It was a small gesture, but she hoped it would discourage Thel's staff from repeating anything they might overhear when she was alone with their employer.

When her butler exited, she picked up Thel's note and cracked open the seal. Inside was a single line of text.

It would be my honor to wear your token.

She flipped the lid on the box and removed her chain from the plush, velvet interior. When she had it coiled in her hand, however, there were still glints of silver inside the box. She dug her fingers into the slippery fabric and removed two diamond teardrop earrings. She fastened them in place and admired the sparkling stones in her dressing mirror. There were more elaborate pieces in her jewelry box, many that were gifts from past lovers, but none of them had ever made her feel so cherished.

The soft, gray gown laid out on her bed would not suffice.

She needed something that would tell Thel exactly how much she appreciated him. She flew to her wardrobe and sorted through her dresses until she found one she had not worn in years. It was a silky, silver confection of organza and cream, silk taffeta with white, bobbin lace trim, from the trailing end of her two years in mourning. She placed it on her bed and added a diamond and pearl necklace and her favorite white silk slippers.

She was about to summon her maid when she remembered the chain. Her staff was used to her eccentricities, but there were aspects of her personal life she kept secret. Even a tiny spark of impropriety could be fanned by rumors into a scandal.

She did not need to add any fuel to the inferno already burning around her.

At least she did not have to worry about choosing the stage for their next confrontation. Her invitation to Saffron's *afternoon of music, at home*, sat propped against her mirror, having arrived earlier that week.

It had been with tremendous guilt that she had imposed upon her friend the favor of extending additional invitations to Mr. Ringwell and Mr. Dawson. She was not certain either would attend, but she had to try.

Thankfully, both Saffron and her intimidating husband were eager to play a part in revealing Mr. Dawson's true nature to Constance, and their event was small enough that the Duke and Duchess of Hestia were unlikely to have heard of it.

Thel's insistence on hiding Constance's engagement from her grandparents felt like a futile gesture, given how quickly news spread in society, but Constance was not her daughter, and therefore, she bowed to his judgment.

She selected her largest reticule and added the invitation to it, along with a heavy bag of coins. They were the bait for her trap. Her skill at cards was second only to her ability to bluff. She would draw Mr. Dawson and Constance into a game, and when he was giddy with victory, she would pull the rug out from under him.

She had yet to meet a man who could maintain his composure when bested by a woman.

When—not if—Mr. Dawson exploded, Constance would see what lay beneath his charismatic exterior. If that did not shake the foundation of her belief in him, nothing would.

❧

HOURS LATER, AS she entered Saffron's home, a shiver went down her back. She was not sure if it was from nerves or anticipation. The chain hung heavily between her breasts, shifting with the smallest movement. It was a manner of play the earl had forced her to engage in. She had hated herself for enjoying it, which was every reason for her to reclaim the pleasure as her own. Thel was not likely to tug painfully on her chain to get her to heel.

She removed her hat and handed it to a footman, then made her way to the receiving room. It was immediately clear that she had arrived too early, as Thel was the only other guest present. He stood next to a trio of musicians positioned in front of the bay windows, wearing a black-and-white checkered frock coat and matching trousers. His black hair was slicked back and even his unruly beard had been groomed into submission.

She watched him discreetly adjust his trousers and wondered if he knew keenly she was aware of the ribbon tied around his cock. He had to feel it, as she felt the chain slinking inside her corset.

He looked at her, and even at such a distance, she could see his harsh exhale. He dropped his gaze to her breasts before jerking his head away and clasping his hands behind his back.

She would not let him surrender so easily.

She flicked open her fan and strolled across the room until she was standing beside him with her wrist positioned directly over her bust.

"Good evening, Lady Allen," he said. "I am pleased to see you wore my gift."

She lifted her free hand and touched the back of her ear. "You have discovered my weakness, my lord. I adore beautiful things. I wore the item you returned to me as well."

He looked at her then, but not at her ears. His gaze skipped to the fan held in her hand. "I look forward to reacquainting myself."

He lowered his arm in a flash and brushed it against her breast. The unexpected flash of sensation made her gasp. Her nipples prickled and her breasts throbbed.

The cellist drew his bow over his instrument. She tucked her fan into her pocket. "Perhaps you might join me for a dance."

A dance was perhaps not wise, given the small size and cramped state of the room, but she was certain Saffron would not mind.

"A quadrille?" the cellist asked. "Or a waltz?"

"A waltz," Thel said. He offered his arm, and she took it, forcing herself to take measured steps despite her impatience. They twirled around the green, leather couch and the dark-walnut table, but she waited until they had to make a tight turn to rub the inside of her thigh against his crotch. A harsh inhalation of breath was her reward, and a tightening of his hand on hers.

He drew her close, dragging his elbow along her chest. The pressure sent shocks of pleasure up to her scalp. She got revenge by swirling her skirt so it brushed against the front of his trousers.

By the time the music had ended, her corset felt too tight, and her face was flushed. She quivered with need and the desire to have his large hands between her thighs. He did not show his discomfort, but she could feel it in the tension in his arm and the increasing speed of his steps.

Unfortunately, they did not have a chance to sneak away, as in the next moment, Constance and Mrs. Quill entered the room.

"There you are," Thel said. "I thought you had become lost." He turned to Olivia and added, "I asked Mrs. Quill to join us."

To discourage Constance from sneaking away, Olivia thought.

She couldn't blame Thel, although Constance's sour expression suggested she was not happy at being stymied.

"We were speaking with Lady Briarwood," Mrs. Quill said. "Our hostess had much to say of embroidery techniques that—"

"Lady Allen, have you seen Mr. Ringwell?" Constance interrupted. She looked around the room. "I have yet to see him."

"What have the two of you done now?" Thel asked.

Constance huffed. "I simply wished to ask him if Ginger had her kittens yet. You must allow me to see them."

"Only if you promise not to return with pockets full of squirming felines," he said. "Your grandmother would have a fit."

Olivia bit back a smile. Mr. Ringwell was clever, using Constance's love of animals as a lure. Perhaps the boy had finally realized that his history with Constance gave him an advantage.

"While we wait," Olivia said, "do you fancy a game of reverse?" She waved at a table, where a deck of cards was waiting.

"Excellent idea," Mr. Dawson said, appearing beside Constance so suddenly that the girl gasped.

"Mr. Dawson," Mrs. Quill said, her tone icy.

Constance maneuvered closer to Mr. Dawson, then said, in a loud voice, "Oh, I seem to have forgotten my shawl in the carriage. Could you retrieve it for me, Mrs. Quill? I would not want to catch a chill."

The older woman narrowed her eyes. "I do not remember selecting a shawl."

"I grabbed one right before we left," Constance said. Then she stuck out her lower lip. "Please?"

Mrs. Quill glanced at Thel, who nodded.

"Very well," she said. "I will be back shortly."

After the woman left, they took their seats around the table and Olivia shuffled the cards. Her heart was beating so rapidly that she nearly dropped them and had to re-shuffle when several cards ended up flipped the wrong way. It had been months since she had exercised her skill.

Her first hand was a mix of low values across all suits, which was perfect for her intentions, as was the glint in Mr. Dawson's eyes. She hoped his dislike for her would lend authenticity to her loss.

Constance started by throwing down the two of clubs. Thel added the five and Mr. Dawson the eight. Olivia pulled the four of hearts from her hand and placed it on the table.

"Ah, are you sure?" Thel asked.

She gave him her best wide-eyed stare. "Did I do it wrong?"

He scooted his chair closer. "Let me see your hand. Yes, that's what I thought. The leading suit was clubs, and you have several. You must play one of those."

"Oh, I see," she said. She replaced her card on the table with the ten of clubs. "That means I win this one, right?"

"Yes," Thel said. "There were no hearts in that set, so you're safe. But since you won, now it's your turn to start."

The game continued, with Olivia taking most of the tricks. "Luck is not on my side today," she said as she pulled the last of the cards toward her.

It was time to prime the trap. She removed the heavy bag of coins from her reticule and thumped it on the table. "Perhaps we could make this more exciting."

"Yes!" Constance cried. She tugged Mr. Dawson's arm, and he mumbled his agreement, although there was a tensing of his shoulders that belied his apprehension.

A small kerfuffle followed as they distributed the coins, sorted out the bets, and agreed to set the scores back to zero.

When Mrs. Quill returned, a black shawl draped over her arm, she frowned at the table. "Gambling, my lord?"

"You could join us," Constance said, accepting her shawl.

The woman politely declined and settled in a nearby chair to watch.

Then Mr. Dawson dealt, and when Olivia saw her hand, she quickly slid three of her coins into the center of the table.

"Confident?" Mr. Dawson said, matching her bid.

She shrugged. "Perhaps."

Thel and Constance added their bids, and then the game began in earnest.

The amount wagered was only the cost of a new bonnet, but the increasingly stiff way Mr. Dawson laid his cards on the table told her it was more than enough to lure him in.

The game progressed as she'd intended, with Mr. Dawson in the lead until the first heart made its appearance. She grumbled as she drew set after set toward her and when there was only one hand left, she made a show of slapping her king of spades on the table, only to have Mr. Dawson gleefully counter it with the queen of hearts.

She sighed and sank into her seat. "I have a lot to learn, it seems."

Thel squeezed Olivia's thigh beneath the table.

"When I win, I will buy myself a set of watercolors," Constance said as she lost her ace of hearts. "Lady Cowper showed me what one can do with them, and I fancy trying it myself, but they are quite expensive, the good kind from Japan."

Mr. Dawson appeared too busy dragging the coins toward himself to respond.

"Another game?" Olivia asked.

Mr. Dawson tightened his arms around his winnings. "I... should not. I do not have a good history with gambling."

Constance turned her large eyes to her betrothed. "Oh, can we please? I only need a bit more to afford the watercolors."

Mr. Dawson groused but eventually agreed. Sweat beaded on his face as he dealt the cards.

When she picked up her cards, it was to find that fate had smiled upon her again. Mr. Dawson, however, had gone quite pale.

She would not allow him to back down. She carefully stacked ten sovereigns and pushed them forward.

"That's all I have left," Constance complained, even as she met the bet.

Thel did the same. Then it was Mr. Dawson's turn. He

moved each of the ten sovereigns one by one until the center of the table was piled with gold.

She allowed him to relax by taking several tricks in a row. Mr. Dawson's increasing excitement and obvious relief made him seem like he was drunk, although she had not seen him imbibe a single glass since arriving.

When he took his first set of hearts, Mr. Dawson barely reacted. When he took his third, his eyes widened. When they calculated scores, his face went bright red. He removed a handkerchief from his pocket and dabbed his forehead. "Excellent game, Lady Allen. I underestimated you. Would you grant me a rematch?"

Constance shifted in her seat. "Another?"

"Another," Olivia said. "For the entire pot."

Constance gave a dramatic sigh but pushed her scant winnings into the center of the table.

Not wanting to give him the chance to complain, Olivia allowed Mr. Dawson to deal, although Constance gave a huff when her turn was denied.

This time, she did not give Mr. Dawson any time to feel he was in the lead. When the game ended, and she piled her winnings back in her valise, she could practically feel Mr. Dawson vibrating. Even Constance was leaning away from him.

Olivia looked around for Mrs. Quill, but the woman had vanished.

"It's only a game," Constance said, her voice tense.

Mr. Dawson stood so quickly that his chair rattled and fell over and made Constance yelp.

"You... You..." He clenched his fists. "You cheated. That is the only explanation. I could not have been bested by a woman."

"I really wanted those watercolors," Constance whined.

He whipped around. "Cease your complaining, girl!"

Constance's eyes filled with tears.

As if realizing he had overstepped, he smoothed the front of his jacket and smiled. "Please forgive me. I am unaccustomed to losing. I will, of course, buy you whatever you desire if it is within my means."

Olivia was about to throw another verbal barb when Saffron rushed into the room. One sleeve of her gown was askew, and several locks of black hair bobbed around her face.

Olivia stood and met her friend. "What is it?" She had not seen Saffron so upset since the morning of her wedding when she had become so overcome with nerves that she had fainted.

"I could not refuse her," Saffron said. "You must understand. It would be the height of rudeness. I've rearranged the seating for dinner, but I was uncertain if this would disrupt your plans..." She put her hand on her chest. "I am overwrought. A moment, please."

Olivia waited as her friend regained her composure, while wondering who could have arrived at the party to put Saffron into such a fit. Her friend was the most organized, capable person she had ever met.

Thel sidled closer to them, an act that was not helpful to the still-struggling Saffron. Before Olivia could tell him to back away, Saffron blurted out words that made her go cold.

"The Duchess of Hestia is here."

Chapter Twenty-Two

T HEL MET HIS mother in the entryway, in what was ultimately a futile attempt to send her away before she shattered their plans.

"How did you find me?" he asked. It would have been a rude question, even in private, but he was beyond caring. He had told the rest of his family that they were taking a carriage ride into the country. No one should have come looking for him.

His mother tutted. "You are a terrible liar, Thellusson. I knew you were lying the moment you told me about your plans for the day." She put her hands on her hips. "You are not the only person in the family who has noticed a change in Constance. When we return home, you will tell me what you have been doing, and why you felt the need to lie, so I am not forced to interrogate poor Mrs. Quill."

He stifled a curse. As was typical of his mother, she'd responded without answering his question, turning the conversation against him.

Olivia appeared at his side and dropped into a curtsey. "Good evening, Your Grace. We did not anticipate the pleasure of your company."

His mother sniffed. "Well, if you are here, Lady Allen, it must mean my darling granddaughter is about socializing with her suitors. Excellent. I would like to meet the young men who have been selected as candidates. To confirm for myself that they are suitable."

It could not possibly get any worse.

Olivia curled her fingers around his arm and uttered a soft, "Oh, no."

"What is it?" he whispered. Then he spotted his daughter and Dawson in the hallway and realized that he had been wrong.

It could absolutely get worse.

Constance moved toward him, apparently unconcerned with how Dawson had exploded with anger only minutes before. It was as if the scenario in the park were repeating, except this time, Dawson was the clear winner and Mr. Ringwell was nowhere to be seen.

When he found the boy, he would have some harsh words to share.

His mother spotted Constance, and he was forced to trail behind as the duchess stalked toward her granddaughter, an unavoidable force. In any other circumstance, the terrified look on Dawson's face when he spotted who was heading toward him might have been entertaining. Unfortunately, Thel did not have time to relish the moment.

"G-Grandmother," Constance said, clutching Dawson's arm. "What are you doing here?"

The duchess folded her arms. "I came to assess your progress regarding your suitors. Do you have a favorite?"

Constance paled. "Well, yes, I suppose."

The duchess switched her attention to Dawson. "And who might you be?"

"This is Mr. Dawson," Constance said.

He gave a deep bow. "Your Grace, it is an honor to meet you."

The duchess narrowed her eyes. "What is your relationship with my granddaughter, Mr. Dawson?"

Thel felt as if he were watching a carriage accident in slow motion. He could do nothing but watch as Dawson brought Thel's carefully laid plans crashing down.

"We are betrothed, Your Grace."

"Indeed?" the duchess asked, lifting her eyebrows. Then she turned to face Thel. "How curious that I am hearing about this for the first time."

He tugged at his cravat. "It's rather complicated."

His mother drew herself up. "I think not. Mr. Dawson, I would be pleased if you would join us for dinner tomorrow night. I am certain the rest of the family would be eager to meet you."

Dawson bowed. "It would be my honor, Your Grace."

The duchess swished her skirts and made for the receiving room. Before the day was out, every member of his household would know that Thel had hidden Constance's engagement from them. The fracture lines that had formed the day he had refused Felix's request to use Constance as part of a business deal would deepen, and soon the family he had fought so hard to unify would fall to pieces.

He felt like Odysseus caught between the six-headed monster Scylla and the whirlpool of Charybdis. He either allowed Constance to marry Dawson, or obeyed the will of his brothers and allowed her to be married off to a stranger.

He couldn't do it. No matter which he chose, he would lose his daughter, perhaps forever. There had to be some other option, some possibility he'd not yet considered that would not lead to the fracture of his family.

He wouldn't give up until he'd found it.

OLIVIA SLUMPED OVER Thel's desk, letting her arms splay over the edges. She had come to his house that afternoon with all her husband's letters in tow, determined to search through them for the slightest reference of a mistress. But even the letters he'd written to his own family had included no mention of marital transgressions. If she hadn't been well acquainted with her husband's insufferable tendency to keep every scrap of paper he put a pen to, she would have suspected him to have burned the letters that contained the information she needed.

"It's time," Thel said. "Mr. Dawson will be here shortly."

She groaned. "It is too late. I am deceased. Please continue without me."

Icy fingers touched the back of her neck. "You are quite warm for a corpse. I believe I could pose you in a seat."

He wrapped his arms around her waist and hauled her out of the chair. She squealed and kicked her legs until he put her back on her feet. The moment he released her, she flitted across the room and out the door, only slowing when she reached the staircase.

Constance stood at the bottom of the steps, staring at the door. Mr. Ringwell stood by her, dressed in a fetching, brushed wool suit.

"At least he made an appearance this time," Thel said when he joined her. There was more than a little bitterness in his tone. Olivia could not blame him. Far from recoiling from her inappropriate suitor after Mr. Dawson's show of anger, Constance had become even more infatuated. They couldn't even have the brief respite of home, as there was no longer a reason for her to avoid speaking of him now that her relatives were aware of her betrothal.

Olivia's hopes to separate the couple were dimming by the day. Constance had shown little interest in anyone but Mr. Dawson and Mr. Ringwell. The former for obvious reasons and the latter because her history with her childhood friend had so far prevented her from cutting him outright.

There was another knock at the door, softer this time. Constance darted forward. She flung open the door and took Mr. Dawson's arm, all but dragging him inside. The slight smile on Mr. Dawson's face did not waver until Mr. Ringwell stepped forward to greet him. Then his smile vanished.

"Mr. Ringwell," Mr. Dawson said icily.

Mr. Ringwell gave a slight incline of his head before Constance pulled Mr. Dawson into the ballroom, where the rest of her family waited.

Thel and Olivia followed, and as such were able to view each family member's reaction when they saw Mr. Dawson.

The duchess's eye twitched. Thel's brothers glowered. Their wives hovered behind them, chatting and acting as if they were not part of the party.

Except for one.

A blonde woman in a gold gown stood apart, glaring at Olivia with such a fierce expression of hatred on her face that it took her aback.

"Don't mind Celina," Thel said. "Felix had his own plans for Constance's future and when I refused to cut ties with you, I fear she was the one who suffered."

Olivia was not so sure. When she turned, it was as if she could feel the woman's gaze digging into her back.

As they took their places around the table, she was relieved to find she was sitting far from the woman.

A bell chimed, and a line of servants entered the drafty dining hall. A shallow bowl of tomato-based soup was placed in front of her. She picked up the appropriate spoon and took a sip, but the texture was too thick for her liking.

"Mr. Dawson," the duchess said from the head of the table. "My daughter has told me of your family's business. I confess some interest. There aren't many men of business in our family."

The slight insult did not appear to bother Mr. Dawson, although Constance's cheeks turned a deep shade of red.

"My father left most of the labor to our trusted employees in America," Mr. Dawson said.

"He sent you away, did he?" the duke asked. He harrumphed. "Not much of a father to ship his son off and split the family apart."

Mr. Dawson shifted in his seat. "He was not well and did not wish me to witness his decline."

"Oh, dear," the duchess said. "William, apologize at once. You know as well as I that you would have done the same in the elder Mr. Dawson's position."

The duke grumbled an apology, which Mr. Dawson gracefully accepted.

The duchess leaned back in her chair with a smile. All evidence so far suggested she approved of Mr. Dawson, who had displayed impeccable manners.

"I did not think the rail business was terribly profitable," Thel's brother, Lord Felix Vaith, said.

"On the contrary, several of my father's business ventures have proven quite lucrative," Mr. Dawson said.

Lord Felix aggressively cut through his chicken. "Indeed? I had thought that the enormous workforce necessary to operate such a business would result in thin margins."

Mr. Dawson shook his head. "Not at all, Lord Felix. However, I would not want to sour the appetites of the ladies present. Perhaps we could discuss this after dinner."

Bright spots of red appeared on Lord Felix's cheeks. "Yes. Of course."

Olivia looked back and forth between the two men. Something about the tone of their voices struck her as false, as if they were having a separate conversation from what she was hearing.

When the second course, a chicken fricassée served with new potatoes, appeared, she leaned over to whisper in Thel's ear. "This is not going well."

"If I may be so bold," Mr. Dawson said suddenly, "I understand that all of you have concerns regarding my intentions toward Constance, but I assure you that despite what you might have heard"—he glanced at Olivia—"I am an honorable man. My only desire is to ensure Constance is happy."

The duchess put her hand on her chest. "Oh, dear. I suppose it was terribly rude of us to put you on the spot."

Mr. Dawson inclined his head. "You are invested in the well-being of your granddaughter, Your Grace. Anyone would have done the same in your position." He paused for a moment before his gaze settled on Olivia. "However, there is one matter that confuses me. As Constance and I have an agreement, why must there be a matchmaker present?"

The room went so silent that the patter of rain on the windows could be heard, as well as clanging and bubbling from the kitchen.

"Mr. Dawson is right," Lord Felix said. "I, for one, have settled my opinion."

"I would rather not spend another second in her presence," Felix's wife said.

Mr. Dawson looked at Thel. "Lord Lowell, does your personal attachment to this woman outweigh the desires of the rest of your family?"

Olivia stared at Thel, waiting for him to respond. When he did not, pressure built behind her eyes until she could no longer stand it. She shoved back from the table and rushed from the room.

Thel might not see the cruelty behind Mr. Dawson's cool façade, but she did. The moment they were married, and Constance could no longer escape, Mr. Dawson would drop his act and become like the earl. Demanding. Possessive. More a prison guard than a husband.

She wished she'd let Thel challenge him to a duel, because then at least it would be over.

She came to a halt as she reached the front door, a plan crystalizing in her mind.

Thel couldn't challenge him, but she could.

She would write another article in her guise as a gentleman, this time demanding the writer provide proof of his claims against her. At the same time, she would casually remark in front of several of her servants that she needed to destroy several important documents related to her marriage that she was storing in her office. If her suspicions were correct, Mr. Dawson was bribing one or more members of her staff to gather information to use against her. He would learn of the documents, and, feeling compelled to produce proof, would try to steal them.

"Olivia, wait," Thel said from behind her.

She spun around, anger forgotten. "I know how we can stop him."

Thel shoved his hands in his hair. "No more plans. No more lies. Mr. Dawson might not be the most appropriate choice, but he has my brother's approval. Constance loves him. It's over."

The damned man was going to sentence his daughter to a life of abuse because he couldn't see beyond his fantasies. She grabbed his wrists. "Stop this nonsense, Thel. Love isn't some magical force that will save Constance from a life of misery. Don't be so childish."

He stepped back, shoving her hands away. "That's what you think of me? That I'm childish?"

His words slipped between his ribs and dug into her heart, but she would not give up while there was a chance to convince him. "You're only seeing what he wants you to see."

"What about the things we've done together?" he asked. "Were they merely games?"

"Thel, listen to me! We can still beat him. I can use the divorce petition to—"

He held up his hand. "That won't be necessary. I apologize, Lady Allen, but your services are no longer required."

Chapter Twenty-Three

RESPONSE TO ACCUSATIONS. The author who has graced this paper over the past week is nothing more than a jealous miscreant intent on disrupting the reputation of a respectable woman who cared for her husband until his dying breath.

Why should we believe a man who makes baseless accusations threaded through with obvious malice and jealousy and provides nothing but his own assurances to back up his claims?

In sum, show us your proof, sir, or still your tongue forever.

OLIVIA CROUCHED BENEATH her desk, waiting for the door to open and her adversary to reveal himself. It had been hours and still there was no sign of Mr. Dawson. She dearly hoped it would not be another wasted night. She was growing tired of spending her evenings alone.

She would much rather be in Thel's bed.

But that was impossible now. He had cut her out of his life two weeks prior without hesitation, choosing to believe in fantasy instead of logic, and she had no one to blame but herself. She had held back the full extent of her feelings against the chance that he shared the same temperament as her former husband, even though everything he had said and done had been proof of the opposite. She'd tried so hard to erase Lord Allen from her mind, but it seemed the damage he'd done was too extensive. He would haunt her for as long as she lived.

She shifted slightly. Her head pounded and her ankles throbbed. Had she been clear enough in her response to encourage Mr. Dawson to act? She was making a huge number of assumptions: that Mr. Dawson would read her response, that he would be provoked enough to act, that he had someone listening inside her household who had passed along her hints.

She touched the bulge in her pocket that held one of the first items she'd procured after her husband's death.

A muzzle-loaded revolver.

One that she would not hesitate to use on Mr. Dawson if he did not agree to her terms. She no longer cared what happened to her if it meant saving Constance. She would gladly sacrifice what was left of her haunted existence to stop Mr. Dawson from hurting anyone else.

Finally, a sound. A creaking from somewhere in the house.

She tensed.

Another creak, louder and closer. Someone was walking down the hallway. She leaned against the underside of the desk and peered through the small hole she had drilled through it. Mr. Dawson, or whomever he'd sent to do his bidding, would not get past her.

The door opened, inch by inch. A figure stepped inside, holding a candle and wearing a dark-blue servant's uniform with a hooded cloak that obscured their features.

Walk closer, she thought. She had left the curtains open so that the person would have to step into the light from the streetlamps. She would wait for them to reach for the latch, then walk behind them and press the revolver to their head.

The figure crossed the room on soft feet, and as Olivia had predicted, stepped into the light cast from the window. When Olivia saw the girl's face, she shot to her feet.

"Willow? What are you doing here?"

The maid squeaked and fumbled for the brass candleholder. Olivia caught it from her before the drapes lit on fire.

"M-My lady," the maid stammered. "I-I was only..." her

lower lip trembled. "I didn't want to do it. Please don't report me."

Olivia sighed. "I won't." She couldn't take her anger out on an innocent girl. Mr. Dawson had bested her again. She reached into her pocket and withdrew several bills, a fraction of what she had gathered to convince Mr. Dawson to leave the country. She pressed them into the maid's hand. "You will have more when your task is complete."

The maid's eyes widened as she clenched her fingers around the bills, which represented several years' worth of standard wages. She could find a new position or buy a small cottage in the country if she wished. It was a life-changing amount of money, and it had the desired effect.

"What do you wish me to do?" the maid asked.

"Take me to your employer."

⁂

OLIVIA'S CARRIAGE RATTLED up to a familiar house. She was still reeling from the knowledge she'd extracted from the maid, but she could not disassemble until the confrontation was over.

She exhaled a long breath before exiting the carriage, then flipped up the hood on the cloak she had borrowed from Willow and found the rear entrance. Once inside, she shuffled into the kitchen, which was bustling despite the late hour. The clang of dishes and the sound of chopping surrounded her. She kept her head down and walked with purpose until she reached the stairs. She hefted her skirts and climbed until her armpits were damp. Then she walked three doors down and knocked. The door creaked open, and a pale face peered out at her. She did not wait for an invitation but shoved her foot into the crack and pushed inside.

A pale woman cowered beneath a blanket on the large bed on the far side of the room.

It was Thel's brother's wife, Lady Felix. Celina Vaith.

"How dare you enter my room?!" Lady Felix shrieked. She threw her blankets off her legs and stood, dressed only in her night rail.

Olivia had her revolver out of her pocket and leveled at Lady Felix before the woman could take another step. The weight of it was reassuring, even as she internally quaked at the knowledge of how much damage it could do. She'd been ready to kill Mr. Dawson, with the certainty that she'd be preventing countless girls from falling into his trap, but she was not sure she could shoot a woman.

Lady Felix's maid sputtered as she backed into the corner, a flimsy pillow clutched in her hands.

"Leave us," Lady Felix said.

The girl darted across the room and exited, letting the door slam shut behind her.

"I assume you caught Willow," Lady Felix said. "Well, if you intend to kill me, do it now before I change my mind."

There was none of the anger Olivia had expected in her tone. It was as if the enemy she'd been prepared to face was nothing more than a fearsome shadow cast by an otherwise innocuous object.

"Why me?" Olivia asked.

Lady Felix's eyes grew distant and misty. "Because he loved me, not you."

The final clue slotted into place. "You were my husband's mistress."

Tears dripped down Lady Felix's cheeks. "He was the most caring man I had ever met. I begged him to leave you. I said I would be happy even if we were poor, as long as we were together. He refused. He said my reputation was more important, and I could not live without it."

Olivia couldn't believe they were discussing the same man. Her husband had never done anything without a purpose. Was it simply that he'd shared all his love with his mistress and there'd been nothing left for his wife?

"It was hard enough watching you go about your life for years after he died," Lady Felix said. "Then you had to go and flaunt your happiness. I couldn't stand watching you get everything you wanted when I miss the earl with every day that passes." She walked over to the hearth and pulled out a fire poker, then brandished it. "It's your fault he's dead!"

Olivia stumbled back, but it took only a few heartbeats for her to recover. Lady Felix's arm trembled so badly, she could barely lift the poker. The woman was not a true threat. She was letting her emotions control her, acting more like a young girl than the woman she was.

Olivia put her rifle away and snatched the poker. The other woman gaped, then rushed to her bed and buried her head in the pillows.

Olivia returned the poker to its place, then walked over to sit on the bed. "The man with whom you fell in love was not the same man who married me. I don't know why you think I killed him, but I assure you he died of consumption."

Lady Felix shook her head. "He wasn't sick. I saw him days before he died, and he was as healthy as I've ever seen him. It was you who killed him, and once I have proof, everyone will believe me. You won't get away with what you've done."

Her words were cruel, but the tone she delivered them in was thin, as if she were grasping on to the last thread of her anger. She reminded Olivia of a feral kitten, hissing fiercely and puffing herself up to make herself appear more threatening. Lady Felix was to be pitied, not feared. Like Thel, she'd believed a falsehood.

"The earl did not want anyone to know he was unwell," Olivia said. She remembered how he had barked commands the morning before he had taken to his bed, how he had shouted at anyone who'd come near. It had driven their housekeeper to tears.

"I saw him," Lady Felix said weakly. "I spoke to him. He was fine."

"You saw what he wanted you to see."

Olivia fell back onto the bed with a sigh, shoving Lady Felix's legs out of her way. "He was kind to me, at the beginning. I understand why you loved him. He could be wonderful when he wanted to be. But there was darkness in him."

Lady Felix scooted down and lay beside her. It was distinctly odd, being so close to her nemesis. She could feel the warmth of Lady Felix's body against her side. They had so much in common. In another life, they might have been friends, or even more.

"I miss him," Lady Felix said, tears heavy in her voice. "I miss him every day. I can't speak of it with Felix or anyone else. You truly did not kill him?" She sounded like she wanted it to be true, at odds with the violence in the articles.

"I didn't kill him," Olivia said. "But I wish I had."

The truth sat between them like a dead thing.

"Why send Mr. Dawson after Constance?" Olivia asked. "The girl is your niece. Was that another way you intended revenge?"

Lady Felix sighed. "That wasn't my idea. Felix committed the girl's dowry to Mr. Dawson as part of a business deal. When Felix could not fulfill his end of the bargain..." She shrugged. "I suppose Mr. Dawson took matters into his own hands."

Thel's entire family had plotted against him. She did not look forward to telling him.

"You told him things, though," she said. "Secrets the earl shared with you. My intention to divorce."

Lady Felix winced. "I was lonely. He listened. Can you blame me?"

Olivia remembered how she had felt, trapped in her house, with only the occasional servant to speak to when the earl had been angry. Given a sympathetic ear, she would have done exactly what Lady Felix had.

"I'm sorry I wrote those things," Lady Felix said. "I was... upset. I hid my correspondence in Constance's room so Felix wouldn't find out and used Thel's title to convince the editor to publish them." She twisted on her side and looked at Olivia. "Is your reputation damaged beyond repair?"

Olivia snorted. "Not nearly."

She had to turn away cards from a dozen men every night. She would know she was truly ruined when the risk of being seen with her outweighed the benefit of her rumored charms.

"I'll recant my statements," Lady Felix said. "I'll... I'll tell Thel everything."

Olivia rolled off the bed and stretched. The night had gone far better than she'd expected. Her reputation would be restored, and she could resume matchmaking. So why wasn't she elated?

Chapter Twenty-Four

THEL TILTED HIS crystal glass back and forth, clinking the ice inside. A fortnight had passed since he'd dismissed Olivia, and a day had not passed without him thinking about her. She'd filled his heart with joy, had taught him things about pleasure and about himself that he might not have discovered otherwise. She was brave, caring, and deserving of a far better life than the one she'd been given.

But they could not be together.

He'd allowed her personal desires to rule him once, and it had earned him nothing but heartbreak. Things might've been different if she'd loved him, but she had been clear on that point. She didn't believe in love. For the sake of his household, he had to let her go.

He leaned back from the stack of papers on his desk. He had not left his office since the previous night, and the sky outside his window was bright. As he stood, his knees cracked, and his back gave a warning twinge. When he sniffed his underarms, the smell was terrible.

Perhaps it had been more than one night.

He summoned a footman and arranged for a bath. When he was clean and dressed again, he poured another measure of brandy and summoned his brother to his office.

Felix opened the door and stepped inside. "You wished to see me?"

Thel could see the satisfaction in his brother's eyes. That was the nature of his family. They were so close that it was very difficult to keep secrets.

Except Constance. She had hidden the most important secret of her life.

None of this would have happened if Marguerite were still alive.

He felt as if someone had burned out his insides and left only ash behind. He'd done his best for his daughter but had failed time and time again. As he could not be the father she needed, she deserved a mother. A feminine hand that could guide her where he could not.

"You know why I called you," Thel said. "You were right. It's time for me to remarry."

Felix gave a wide smile. "Excellent. There are several fine ladies who would suit. Do you have any preferences?"

Felix was tall and confident, with a penchant for matchmaking.

Thel waved his hand. "Her experience and breeding are all that matter. This household needs a woman who knows what she is about."

Felix raised an eyebrow. "A widow, perhaps? There are not many of those, but I can think of several who would be amenable."

Lady Allen was a widow. She had befriended Constance, sought only to ensure his daughter's happiness, and he had thrown her out of his house for it.

"A widow will suffice," he said.

"Excellent," Felix said. "There is Lady Newberry, of course, although she is a bit stern. You might prefer Lady Rothwellan…"

Thel listened halfheartedly. He didn't care whom Felix chose to be his wife. All that mattered was that she could fulfill her marital duties and produce an heir. Beyond that, it didn't matter what she looked like or even if she carried on her own affairs outside of their marriage.

His dreams, his very thoughts, were devoted to Olivia. Every sound was her deep laugh, every crack the sound of her heels on the floor. The sooner he married, the sooner he could put her behind him.

Or so he hoped.

THEL PUT HIS chin in his hand and leaned his elbow on the padded arm of the upholstered settee in his mother's sitting room, trying not to think about how much he felt like a child preparing to be disciplined, and not a five-and-forty-year-old man. He was not in the habit of spending his mornings being lectured, but the note his mother had placed on his desk had left no room for argument. His family was already coming apart. He could not afford any additional conflict. Thus, he waited.

"I cannot abide this," his mother said as she dabbed her face with a piece of cloth. "Have I taught you nothing, Thel? You cannot simply pick a woman to marry at random!"

Of course that was why she'd summoned him. Felix had informed her of his intention to remarry. His brother had a terrible habit of not keeping his mouth shut.

"I am not choosing at random, Mother. I am carefully weighing the benefits of each candidate. I am not interested in locking myself into a spiteful marriage, as my brother did."

His brother had had set his sights on Lady Celina the very day she'd debuted, claiming she was the most beautiful woman he had ever met. Thel had tried to talk Felix out of marrying the woman so quickly, but his brother had refused to listen.

His mother shook her head. "Your brother is a fool. If he had truly known his own heart, he would not have pursued Celina with such haste." She picked up a framed portrait of his father on the table and smiled. "Love does not flower in an instant like a night-blooming rose, my dear. You must tend the bud of your love and allow it to grow, showering it with affection." She put the portrait down. "Do not look at me with such sad eyes. You have a chance at a life your brother could only imagine." She sniffed. "He would never admit it, of course. He is as stubborn as your father."

Thel clenched his hands in his lap. "You and Father did not have to wait."

His mother put her hand on his back. "Oh, Thel. I should have told you years ago, but your father insisted we maintain the fairy tale. My marriage was arranged."

Thel felt as if someone had kicked him in the chest. His whole life he had believed that his parents had fallen in love over a whirlwind weekend, that they had married within days of meeting and then had a fulfilling life filled with laughter and children.

He had never questioned the story, even as his brothers had teased him. He had clung to the fairy tale throughout his adolescence and his courtship of Marguerite. Finding out that it was not true made something deep inside him crack, and then shatter.

"I should have arranged Constance's marriage from the start," he said.

His mother grabbed his cheeks. "Listen here, Thel. I will not have you acting the fool. Your brother has done more than enough of that." She dropped her hands. "I despised your father in the beginning. He was a cold man. The only time he revealed his true self was in our bed."

Thel cleared his throat. "Mother, I would rather not hear—"

She chuckled. "Yes, yes, a man does not want to know of his mother's bed play. I understand. The point remains valid. Your father and I fell in love over time. Friendship blossomed between us first, before turning to affection, and finally love. The story I gave you was true, although accelerated. It was not days, but months. Your father slowly revealed more of himself to me, and I did the same." She sighed. "If love could be found so easily, there would be far fewer matchmakers operating in London. Much like that woman you were involved with. What became of her?"

"I dismissed her."

His mother's eyebrows rose. "Why?"

"I didn't want her to disrupt the family." Before his mother could argue, he barged ahead. "Your story only emphasizes that I should not allow Constance to marry Mr. Dawson. Like Felix, when the attraction wanes, she will not be able to sustain her happiness. She'll be trapped. Is that not what you meant?"

His mother sniffed. "My marriage was arranged, and it ended happily for me. But that does not mean all such marriages are successful. It takes complementary personalities, trust, and friendship. A successful matchmaker looks beneath the surface to the core of a person. However, I do not believe Constance is ready to marry. She must have time to explore herself before she commits to a man."

"Perhaps I was too impatient," he said. "She should not have had her debut so soon."

He had been so focused on securing Constance's future and fulfilling his promise to his wife that he had not considered she was not ready. Once again, he'd allowed his own desires to cloud his judgment.

His mother snorted. "It's a miracle. You are finally coming to your senses."

He slouched on the couch. "I thought I was doing right by her."

Constance had wanted so desperately to grow up that he had been unable to resist her demands. He should have insisted on a gradual introduction into society. Instead, he had allowed her to dive in without proper education or training. It was no wonder she had floundered.

"I failed her," he said.

His mother groaned. "You are a troublesome child, Thellusson. You take the weight of the world on your shoulders. I am as much to blame as you. I recognized the signs but did not interfere, even when it became apparent she was corresponding with someone." Her expression softened. "Love grows in many ways, my son."

A rap on the door interrupted them.

"Come in," his mother said.

Constance entered, a frown on her face. Mrs. Quill stood behind her, and it was clear from the older woman's posture that it was only her presence that was keeping Constance from fleeing.

"Hello, Grandmother," Constance said. She did not meet Thel's gaze, nor acknowledge that he was present.

The duchess smiled. "My dear Constance. You wound your father."

Constance's frown deepened. "I do not wish to speak to him. He sent Lady Allen away."

He sank into the couch. In his attempt to save his daughter from heartbreak, he'd turned her against him.

Mrs. Quill pushed Constance forward. The girl staggered into the room, then perched on the edge of a seat across from her grandmother.

"I have discussed the matter of your marriage with your father," the duchess said. She picked up the teapot and poured a measure into a cup, then passed it to Constance. The girl accepted it gracefully and held it above the saucer. She did not toss it back in one swoop, or dollop it with sugar, or grab a cookie from the tray on the table.

Where had his little girl gone? He did not recognize the woman before him. He was so used to seeing her as a child. She had grown up when he had not been looking.

The duchess drank her tea and then picked up a biscuit and took a bite. Throughout, Constance remained silent.

"Very good," the duchess said finally. She looked at Thel. "I was remiss in not educating my son in the way of women."

Thel cringed but recognized that it was his turn. "Constance, I will not give my blessing for you to marry Mr. Dawson."

Constance's fingers turned pale on her teacup, but she did not speak. That was already an improvement over the pouting and whining he'd expected.

"Do you at least understand why I do not approve?" he asked. This was the chance she had to reveal if she had learned anything from Olivia's lessons. Could she separate herself from her situation and analyze it critically, or had Dawson corrupted her mind so thoroughly that she was blind to his flaws? If so, then Thel would have to take more drastic action. He was prepared to spirit them to the new world if it came to that.

Constance stared into her tea. "John makes me feel like I am the most important and beautiful woman in the world." She jutted her chin forward. "He might not be perfect, but I don't want to give up on him. He's already agreed to wait until I am one-and-twenty."

He wanted to shout at her that the fortune Dawson claimed was a falsehood, but she had to discover the truth on her own. Otherwise, she might believe he was manipulating the facts, or her mind. Her acceptance to wait was a stalemate, one he would accept.

"That is sufficient," he said.

Constance smiled, and he saw some of the girl she had been in her eyes. The girl who'd danced in the flower beds and challenged the staff to duels with brooms instead of swords. He hadn't seen that girl since they'd arrived in London, unless Olivia had been around. She'd drawn the fun out of Constance, and out of him, too. He missed that, missed seeing Olivia smile and following along with her whims. She was the most remarkable woman he had ever met.

And he had chased her from his house.

"Perhaps we should discuss *your* prospects next, Father?" Constance asked.

His mother nodded. "Yes, we should. He has made a rather foolish mistake."

"Quite right," Constance said. "I believe it is time I make decisions on his behalf, as he has been doing for me."

He looked back and forth between them. "Are you referring to Lady Allen? Wait, no." He laughed. "Of course you are. What else would you be talking about? I must agree. I was foolish."

The clouds cleared in his mind. It didn't matter that Olivia did not love him. His mother had not loved his father when they married, but they had developed friendship and affection, which had bloomed into love. He could have that, too.

If she was willing to give him another chance.

❧

THEL SHOULD HAVE been on his way to Olivia's house, but fear kept him trapped in his seat. What if Olivia refused to see him? He didn't want her simply in his bed. He wanted to wake up every morning to see her smile, to dance with Constance, to pretend to be knights or princesses or whatever struck their fancy. Marguerite's death had gouged a hole in his heart that had never properly healed, but he felt ready to move on.

"Thel?"

Thel jerked upright. Felix's wife stood in the doorway with her hands clasped at her waist.

"Celina," he said. "Is something the matter?"

She had never come to his office before. His mind immediately jumped to the worst possibility, and he rushed forward to meet her. "Is it the children? Has something happened to Alanna or Bennett?"

She shook her head. "No. I...I've come to confess." She removed a handkerchief from her sleeve and dabbed at her cheeks, although he saw no tears.

"Confess what?" he asked.

"It's all my doing." Her chin trembled. "I-I wrote the letters. I used your title to convince the *London Evening Standard* to print them. I told the police that Lady Allen murdered her husband."

He felt as if she had punched him in the chest. "You did *what?*

177

Why?"

She dropped her gaze to the floor. "The Earl of Allen and I were in love."

"You and the earl," he said slowly. The news was such a shock that he was having trouble putting together sentences. He imagined Celina hunched over her writing desk, writing furiously, a scowl across her face. Olivia had been so sure it was Dawson, and he had believed her.

"Then who—" he started before Celina began speaking again.

"Felix is the one who sent Mr. Dawson after your daughter. My husband promised Constance's dowry to Mr. Dawson in exchange for some"—she threw up her hands—"business deal. I haven't the faintest idea of the details. He is the one who convinced all the other matchmakers to turn you away. Now, if you will excuse me, brother." She tilted her head up. "I have one final article left to commission." Then she spun and left him standing in the middle of his office, his mind whirling.

Felix.

He had been so secure in his leadership over his family that he had failed to consider that his own brother was acting against him. But the blame could not be solely placed on Felix. Thel had dismissed his brother's objections, hoping that Constance would find the same happiness that her parents and grandparents had found. Once again, he had allowed his own desires to outweigh the will of his brothers, and the result had been a disaster.

It would not happen again.

He would find Felix and set things right between them, then he would go to Olivia's house and apologize for how he had treated her. If she was willing to be his wife, they would be married as soon as he could arrange it. He already had the special license he'd procured before he'd asked her to marry him the first time. All she had to do was say 'yes.'

Chapter Twenty-Five

RECANT OF PRIOR STATEMENTS. I wish to make my official apology to Lady Allen, wife of the deceased Earl of Allen. Lady Allen has shown nothing but grace and kindness to any soul who enters her orbit, and it is with a heavy heart that I admit any accusations placed against her have been falsified. The late Lord Allen was not poisoned but passed peacefully in his sleep after a long battle with consumption. Any further accusations should be met with the toughest of skepticism. You will hear no more from me.

"LADY ALLEN, WILL you be attending Lady Fairweather's ball?"

"Oh, Lady Allen, who is your modiste?"

"Are you free for the next dance, Lady Allen?"

Olivia struggled to keep the smile on her face as the crowd pressed in on her. She should have been ecstatic. She had, after all, done what she had sought to do. Lady Felix had published her retraction, and as a result, the entire *ton* wanted her to attend their events, or find a husband for their daughter, or judge their art competition.

"Yes, I will be attending Lady Fairweather's ball," she told the woman to her left. Then she swiveled her head and found a wide-eyed debutante. "A lovely Parisian woman named Madame Julian designed this gown. I am certain she would appreciate your patronage." Finally, she addressed the Earl of Bellows. "I am parched, my lord. Could you fetch me a glass of champagne?"

The man raced off to do her bidding, and she was not surprised when two dandies quickly took his place.

They were only willing to entertain her as long as she could provide them with what they wanted: mentorship, popularity, attention. The moment she fell out of favor, they would vanish like birds spooked by the sound of a shot.

Even Thel had come to her wanting her patronage for Constance, of whom she had not seen a hair since her fight with the marquess. She dearly wanted to know if Constance had still committed herself to Mr. Dawson, but she did not dare send another missive, as Thel had returned her first unopened.

She was not naïve enough to believe she could change his mind. He was just like the earl, presenting one face to society while behaving entirely differently in private.

The same way you adopt the role of Lady Allen?

She chased the voice away and concentrated on Lady Deirdre, who shoved a black-haired waif forward. The girl's eyes were enormous in her narrow face. She was pretty, although with a pinched look about her, as if she had never had enough to eat.

It was not an unlikely scenario. The newest fad for girls was swooning, which was seen as graceful. In reality, it did nothing except make them more fragile and easier for the men of society to manage.

Olivia bared her teeth in what she hoped was a reassuring smile. "I apologize, but my schedule is quite full."

She could not take another girl under her wing and risk repeating what had happened to Constance and Lady Mason. It would break what was left of her heart.

She searched the crowd without realizing for whom she was looking, and when she spotted Constance, the shock startled a gasp from her lips. The girl was surrounded by men and women chattering away to get her attention.

Lord Bellows returned at that moment with her champagne. She downed it, held up the glass for a passing servant to take, then took her savior's arm. "I desire some fresh air."

The man smiled. "Of course, Lady Allen. Perhaps I could call you 'Olivia'?"

"If that is your wish, my lord." She did not care what he called her. She just had to get out of the ballroom before Thel, who had to be present if his daughter was, saw her. The jagged edges of the wound he had sliced across her heart had not yet come together. She had spent each night since their fight replaying the moments leading up to her dismissal, imagining what she might have said to change the inevitable outcome.

When they reached the hedge maze, she relaxed her death grip on Lord Bellows's arm. She was safe. Thel was unlikely to venture so far from the ballroom. The gardens were the domain of lovers, not uptight men who insisted on believing in a fantasy. Love. What a ridiculous notion. Even if it existed, she was better off without it. Love brought vulnerability, which led to pain.

"I have been waiting for this day for months," Lord Bellows said. He shoved her against the foliage.

She should have screamed, or struggled, or done anything to fight back, but she had lost hold of Lady Allen. She was only scared, traumatized Olivia. She clenched her eyes shut and waited for it to be over, only to hear a strangled grunt, and then the hands clasped around her upper arms loosened, and she was left leaning into the hedge.

She fluttered her eyelids open. The man cupped his crotch, his face purple, his teeth bared. Constance stood next to him, her fists balled and held at her chin, her eyes narrowed.

"You bitch." Lord Bellows struggled upright. "I'll—"

"Do nothing," Olivia said. "Unless you would like rumors of your inability to perform to become public knowledge. You don't have any children, do you, Lord Bellows?"

He scowled. "You wouldn't dare."

Constance flitted to her side and took her arm. "I would love to hear the story of how Lord Bellows propositioned you but could not stand at attention."

Lord Bellows sputtered but made no further effort to rise.

Olivia squeezed Constance's hand and then drew her out of the hedge maze. They did not need to give the man a chance to change his mind.

"I owe you a debt," Olivia said when they were far enough away from Lord Bellows that she did not worry he would overhear.

Constance plucked the bloom of a carnation, tucked it behind her ear, then did a deep curtsey before Olivia. "I am your most humble servant."

Olivia fell into the game as smoothly as if they had just danced in Constance's room that morning. She picked up a broken stick from the ground and brandished it. "Nonsense. You are my loyal retainer. My bodyguard. Lord Bellows did not stand a chance."

Constance picked up another stick and held it out in a fighting stance. "I believe you need a lesson, lest this incident occur again."

She lunged, and Olivia met the strike, laughter bubbling up in her throat. She slashed and cracked her branch against Constance's in a flurry of blows, falling deeper into the role with each step. This was what she'd missed. This freedom of allowing herself to be and do whatever she wanted. She mock-stabbed Constance in the chest, and the girl let out a dramatic moan.

"You are the one who requires further lessons," she said. Then she tossed the stick, dropping their game in a heartbeat. "Where's Th—your father? I find it hard to believe he let you out of his sight."

Constance bowed her head. "He didn't come. He spends most of his time in his office. I think he misses you."

Olivia sat beside her. "Lord Lowell is no longer my concern. He dismissed me."

"You forgot about him so quickly?"

"Nothing could be further from the truth." She peered up at Constance. "What about Mr. Dawson? Do you still want to marry him?"

Constance pursed her lips. "I love him."

"Are you still giving him money?"

"It's only until his inheritance comes in."

Olivia put a hand on Constance's shoulder. "How can you be sure there *is* an inheritance?"

Tears dripped down Constance's cheeks. "I don't know."

Olivia handed her a handkerchief.

Constance dabbed at her cheeks. "I wish you could see what I see in him. Your blessing means so much to me. You are the closest thing to a mother I have."

The pressure inside Olivia's chest grew until she felt as if she were going to burst. She had meddled in Constance's life from the moment the girl had been introduced to her. She had allowed her own past to cloud her perception of Mr. Dawson. The man had shown signs of cruelty, but that might have been as much her fault, as she had done nothing but antagonize him. She had placed him in the same box as the earl and had resisted any attempts Constance made to show her any other truth.

"I would have been blessed to have a daughter as lovely as you," she said.

Constance gave a hiccupping laugh before handing the handkerchief back. "It's not too late."

Olivia caught the lilt in her voice. The girl was teasing her or playing matchmaker herself. She elbowed her in the ribs. "You are a clever little hellion. What's your scheme? Did you summon your father here to force us into a confrontation?"

Her shoulders drooped. "I tried."

She bit the inside of her cheek. This was certainly another of Constance's manipulations. The girl was determined when there was something she wanted. On the other hand, if she did not intervene, she might find herself caught in a situation with Thel that she did not expect. There was only one way to give Constance the closure she needed and prevent any awkward incidents.

She dreaded speaking to Thel, but perhaps it was for the best. Her duty as matchmaker was over, but if he was willing to apologize, it was still possible that they could have some manner of future together.

"If it would appease you, I will visit the house and speak with your father."

Constance gasped. "Really?"

Olivia tapped the girl on the nose. "Only if you promise to give up any further scheming. You can become a matchmaker when you are older, if you so desire, but you are presently too young to be meddling with the emotions of your elders."

"I'll stop," Constance said. Then she glanced over Olivia's shoulder.

"Well, go on then," Olivia said with a smile. "Mr. Dawson won't wait all night. You're planning on meeting him, are you not?"

Constance had the grace to blush before she scurried into the gardens.

It took a tremendous force of will for Olivia to stop herself from following.

Chapter Twenty-Six

THEL CLENCHED HIS clasped hands between his knees as he perched on the edge of a plush horsehair sofa in Olivia's receiving room. The confrontation with Felix had gone as poorly as he'd expected, with the man refusing to admit he'd done anything wrong. Now Felix was in the process of finding a new residence, but instead of trying to repair his relationship with his brother and prevent his family from fracturing further, Thel was waiting for Olivia to see him.

When he'd arrived, her butler had bustled him inside and vanished. No other staff had entered since. He was beginning to wonder if they had left him here rather than tell him Olivia didn't want to see him. That would explain the drawn curtains and cold fireplace. But he would not leave. As long as he stayed, there was a chance Olivia would forgive him.

If she refused to see him, he would leave, but it would take a long time for him to heal. His love for her had grown through his soul like the roots of a tree. Pruning her from his life would take a significant amount of time and effort.

He stared at the door, willing Olivia to walk through and see him. He would go down on his knees and speak the words from his heart. Even if it was hopeless, he had to try. He was staring so intently that he barely heard the other door opening and the soft gasp that followed. He imagined Olivia bending down before him, picking up his hand and pressing it to her cheek and—

"Thel."

She stood in front of him, her hands clasped at her waist. "I was hoping you would come."

"You were?" This was not going the way he had expected.

"I had just decided to come to you," she said. Then she leaned in and pressed her lips to his. Although shocked for a moment, he quickly tilted his mouth and brought his arms around her waist, pulling her closer. She tasted like strawberries, and the sounds she made as he plundered her mouth drove him wild.

She put her hands on his thighs, shoved them wider apart, and then moved into the space. Her soft stomach pressed against his hardness and made him groan. He ached for her. Having finally experienced what he had long denied himself, he found he longed for more.

When his resistance had been sawed thin, and he was about to heft her in his arms and take her deeper into the house for a proper bed, he withdrew and cupped her face in his hands.

"I love you," he said. "That is what I should have told you when I asked you to marry me. I want you to be my wife not only because we are compatible, but also because I cannot imagine a future without you in it. Marry me."

The following few seconds of silence were some of the longest of his life. If she declined, he wasn't sure there was anything else he could offer her. He had laid all of his cards on the table.

"Yes," she said.

"Thank God," he said. Then he threaded his hands into her hair and drew her in for a deep kiss.

He wanted to feel her spasm around him and then spend himself deep inside her. He wanted to bring her to heights of pleasure she had never experienced. He wanted to bridge the gulf between them and learn everything she knew.

Her bedroom was a good place to start. He'd started to lift her into his arms when a knock came at the door.

Olivia twisted out of his grasp. Her cheeks were flushed, her lips bruised and bright red, her hair falling out of her chignon, but with a few quick movements of her hands, it was as if nothing had happened.

"Come in," she said.

Mrs. Quill entered, looking more disheveled than he had ever seen her.

"Mrs. Quill?" Olivia stepped forward. "What are you doing here?"

"It cannot be what I think it is," Mrs. Quill said. She stumbled a step, looking pale and sweaty. "There must... There must be some other explanation!"

"Take a seat before you faint," Olivia said as she guided the woman toward the couch.

Thel came to kneel in front of Mrs. Quill. Her eyes were so wide that he could see the whites all around her pupils. "What is it?"

"It's your daughter, my lord," Mrs. Quill said. "She's vanished."

⁂

THE TIME BETWEEN leaving Olivia's home and arriving at his own passed for Thel like a blur. When they reached Constance's room, the door was open.

Olivia touched the wood with her fingertips, and it creaked open. Inside, pillows were strewn over the floor, the dressing table was set on its side, and the window was open.

The facts worked their way through his mind. Constance was missing, and her room was chaotic, as if there had been a fight.

He took four long steps over to the cord in the corner of the room and tugged it twice. His butler appeared at the door at once. "My lord?"

The words would not come. The moment he spoke, his worst fear became true. He tried again, clearing his throat, only for Olivia to step between him and the older man.

"Have any carriages approached the house in the last hour?" she asked.

"I don't believe so, Lady Allen." His butler looked around the room, his eyes widening. "I-I will ask the housekeeper and the kitchen staff if anyone saw or heard anything." He spun and left. The sound of footfalls echoed through the hallway, slow at first, before increasing to a rapid pace.

"Where could she have gone?" Thel whispered. He walked over to the bed and picked up the book they had been reading. There was no slip of paper or flower to mark her progress. She always left a bookmark after reading.

"Dawson," he said. When he found the man, he would strangle him.

Constance was a prize too valuable to give up. By encouraging her to take more time to consider her prospects, he had been certain that she would eventually see that Dawson was not the man he claimed to be.

Perhaps Dawson had realized that, too.

His knees buckled, and he grabbed the pillar of Constance's bed to keep from collapsing. He had ruined everything. His daughter would be shackled to a man who cared only about her fortune. Dawson could not afford to allow her to stay within her father's reach. He had to know that Thel would stop at nothing to get her back, even if it meant operating outside the law.

He had to go after them and stop Dawson before he did whatever awful thing he was planning. But where to start?

A hand touched his cheek.

"We will find her," Olivia said.

He gathered her against his chest, and the tight places inside him eased.

The door swung open, and his butler rushed in. "The cook says that a carriage pulled up to the back entrance recently. She only noticed because she thought it was a delivery from the grocer. She watched from the window as two figures entered. They left down the back alley." He cleared his throat. "I'm afraid that's all we have."

"Prepare my carriage," Thel said. Then he turned to Olivia, but before he could say anything, she spoke.

"Do not even suggest that you pursue this without me," she said. "I feel as responsible for this situation as you do."

He put his hands on her upper arms. "This man is dangerous. I don't know what he will do, or where he will go." He knew what she was going to say next, so he barged ahead before she could say it. "I trust your instincts, and I know you can take care of yourself. You've proven that." He remembered the man from the garden, lying prone on the ground. Constance and Olivia were formidable women. If any man tried to do anything they didn't like, he would not get far.

Chapter Twenty-Seven

T HE INN WAS not of a caliber Olivia considered reputable, but given the sheeting rain and the way their carriage had nearly become stuck in the mud several times, she'd agreed when Thel had said it would have to do.

They left their conveyance with the stableboy and dashed across the courtyard and into the small building to be met by the sound of clinking beer glasses and fiddle music. The savory smell of mutton and roasting onion and garlic tickled her senses, making her mouth water. She had not taken a proper afternoon tea before they had set out.

A plump woman wearing a stained apron approached them. "What can I do for you?" She wiped her hands with a thin cloth.

"Do you have a room for…" Olivia started, before realizing her conundrum. She glanced at Thel, who shrugged, then looked back at the proprietress. "My husband and I?"

Saying the words gave her a thrill.

"Aye, we have one," the woman said. "Connor, take them up to the room above the kitchen." She winked at them. "Always warm that one, no fear of drafts. We don't get many toffs."

They followed a lanky boy to a dusty room that had a bed that would barely fit them both but was better than spending the night in their carriage.

Thel sat down on the bed, and it made an ominous creaking noise.

She sat beside him. "Worried about Constance?"

"I didn't... I should have prepared her more."

She put her arm around his shoulders and squeezed. "You did the best you could. No one could have predicted that he would suddenly abscond with her."

When he shot her an incredulous look, she sighed. "I suppose it was not all that unlikely, but that does not mean it is your fault. If you are to blame anyone, blame Mr. Dawson."

The tips of his fingers were turning white. "They might already be at Gretna Green. What do we do if we get there too late?"

She could not answer that because she shared similar concerns. She had tried to express them to Thel in the carriage, but he had not listened, or perhaps had not heard. He was so focused on recovering his daughter that he had not been receptive to her words.

"We will achieve nothing by sitting here," she said. "Let us find out what that remarkable smell was. It has been an age since I have had simple fare. My cook is rather fond of elaborate dishes."

This at least got a chuckle out of him, which was an improvement. She squeezed him once more before following him downstairs.

The noise in the main room was overwhelming, but she focused on the smell of the mutton pie and fresh bread the proprietress placed in front of her when she sat down. It was better than adequate, which explained why it was so busy, when they were far from the nearest town.

Thel consumed his meal in such regular bites that she wondered if he was even tasting it. When he finished, he slid his empty plate away and put his elbows on the table.

"Do you think they came through here?" she whispered. It was not a main road, but it was the most direct route to their destination.

Thel narrowed his eyes. "Perhaps."

When he did not elaborate, she tried again. "I'll ask if anyone has seen them." She began to rise, but Thel put a hand on her thigh and pushed her back down.

"Being so direct won't do us good," he said. "Look around. Every single person here is aware of us."

She searched the room and was dismayed to find that he was right. At least half of the room was blatantly staring at them, and the other half was alternating between sly glances and carefully averting their gazes.

"Are we safe?" she asked. She had very little experience outside of London. Had they made a mistake by stopping? Traveling at night risked them being accosted by highwaymen.

Suddenly, a man in a robe crossed the room and sat down at their table. "Lookin' for something, guv?"

"A young girl with golden curls. Accompanied by one or more men," Thel said.

The man shoved his arm across the table, palm up.

Thel somehow retrieved several coins from his pocket without making it obvious where he had stashed them. He dropped four shillings in the man's hand. The coins vanished, and the man leaned forward, lowering his voice to a hush.

"I ain't seen the gel, but a toff like you asked the same question, an hour past."

"Is he here?" Thel asked.

The man shook his head. "Upstairs. Fourth door." He grinned, showing several missing teeth. "Planned to rustle him. He looked quite the prize."

Thel slid three more shillings across the table. "Leave him to us."

The man snatched the coins, then rushed out of the inn as fast as he had appeared at their table.

"Who do you think it is?" Olivia asked. "One of your brothers?" She couldn't think of anyone else who could've learned what had happened and followed them so quickly. Although, given Felix's involvement in Constance's predicament, she hoped it was not him.

"Let's find out," Thel said.

They climbed the steps and rapped on the door the man mentioned. Olivia stayed close behind Thel, for fear they would be greeted with a revolver. But when the door creaked open, it wasn't either of Thel's brothers who looked at them with bags under his eyes.

"Mr. Ringwell, what are you doing here?" she asked. Then she laughed. "Oh, I see. You were coming to stop Constance, weren't you?"

Mr. Ringwell rubbed his face with his hands. "I told her Dawson was no good, but she wouldn't listen to me. I couldn't let him take advantage of her anymore. I was on the way to the house, preparing to knock and ask Connie to marry me, when I passed her and Dawson in a carriage." He slumped against the doorframe. "She looked so unhappy. If I had been ten minutes earlier..." He shook his head. "Come inside. Let's talk."

Ten minutes later, with all of them cramped inside the room, Mr. Ringwell gave the rest of his story. He'd followed the carriage on horseback from a distance until they'd stopped at a house.

"I saw inside," Mr. Ringwell said. "It is a shambling place but filled with all manner of valuable items. Dawson locked Constance in a room."

"How was she?" Thel asked. His hands were clenched in the sheets of the bed he sat on, his knees coming up to his chest because the bed was so low to the ground. He tapped his toes on the ground in a rhythm before flushing and stopping. Olivia had no such restraint. Her knees bounced up and down as she listened to Mr. Ringwell's story, his words painting a vivid picture in her mind.

She was acutely aware that if her parents had not given in, she might have ended up in a similar position. She knew that had she been in Constance's place years ago, the earl wouldn't have needed to convince her to abscond.

"Though she was frowning, she appeared well," Mr. Ringwell

said. "I couldn't tell if she was staying with him willingly or if he kidnapped her."

"It won't take long for them to reach Gretna Green and marry," Olivia said.

"Then we have to stop him before that happens," Mr. Ringwell said. "But how? There are others nearby. Highwaymen. He doesn't allow any of them in the house, as if they are an army surrounding the princess in her castle."

"Then we bring our own army," Thel said. "You return and watch Constance. If you get a chance to rescue her without revealing yourself, do it. Otherwise, wait for us to return, and we'll confront him together. Dawson won't get away with this."

OLIVIA SLAMMED HER hands down on the desk. "What do you mean, he's not available?"

Her hair fell into her face. She blew it away from her lips with a puff of air. She could only imagine how awful she looked. They had expected it to be much easier to find someone to come with them to arrest Mr. Dawson for kidnapping, but the first two places they had checked had laughed at their request. When pressed, it became clear that Mr. Dawson had bribed the local law enforcement to ignore his activities.

The man was always one step ahead.

They had split up and taken horses to the outlying communities, hoping to find someone who was not on Mr. Dawson's payroll.

This small hamlet was her best bet, as it was insulated from the nearby towns by a river that made it difficult to sneak in without being seen by the entire town. She had counted upon that, and on her appearance ensuring she would be received without incident. Unfortunately, the sheriff she had been assured was here was not.

They were running out of time. The sun was high in the sky. Dawson would continue to Gretna Green without delay. They might already be—No. That was foolish. She was only digging herself into despair, thinking such things. She had to trust in Mr. Ringwell, watching the house. If something awful happened, he would act.

"We haven't had a sheriff since the last one died," the young man in front of her said. "But if it's a lawman you're after, Mrs. Jeffries, the baker, was saying a constable from the city came to speak to her last night. Maybe he's still about."

"Where would he go next?" Olivia asked. She didn't care how or why a London policeman was about, as long as he was willing to help them.

The boy scratched his chin. "The blacksmith, perhaps? He's got the only other big house hereabouts."

"Thank you," Olivia said before rushing out and mounting her horse. The animal was stubborn as a mule and refused to move faster than a canter but was the only creature she trusted herself to ride in her state of agitation. Breaking her neck would help nothing. Her only other options for mounts had been their carriage horses, which were too large for her to ride safely. She'd been lucky the owner of the inn had been willing to lend her the animal.

She exited the town through the same bridge she had entered and found Thel waiting for her at their rendezvous point. The heavy furrowing of his brow told her everything she needed to know about his success.

"Nothing?" he asked.

She told him what she'd learned, and together, they rode up the hill until a house became visible. As they approached, the door burst open, and a uniformed man stepped out. To Olivia's shock, it was the same constable who had interrogated her at Thel's house.

"You," Thel said.

The constable came up short, his eyes wide. "Lord Lowell.

What are you doing here?"

"We should ask you the same question," Olivia said.

The man's eyes widened further as he took her in. "Lady Allen." Then he scowled. "Are you two involved as well?"

"Involved with what?" Olivia asked.

"Burglaries," he said. "I've tracked a gang of thieves to this area, but they've vanished."

Olivia glanced at Thel. "Could it be…?"

Thel nodded. "Most likely. Constable, I believe we can help each other."

"Thel!" came a new voice. It was Mr. Ringwell, riding up the path on a black mare. He came to a stop next to Thel, and she could tell from the grim look on his face that he did not have good news, either.

"I've been searching for you for hours," Mr. Ringwell said. "Dawson has locked her in the house and left. I tried to approach but was nearly spotted by the guards Dawson set. We must act now! This might be our only chance to get to her before it's too late."

Mr. Smith walked forward. "What's this, then?"

Olivia quickly filled the man in, watching his face grow more tense with every word. When she finished, he cursed and ran for his own horse, tied to the fence.

She could tell Thel wanted to dash off, but there was a flaw in that plan.

One she was certain he would not be happy to hear.

She put her hand on Thel's shoulder. "We have to let Mr. Ringwell rescue her." His scowl prompted her to continue, softer. "If Dawson still has her in his thrall, she's more likely to see you as an intruder than a savior." That was how she'd seen her parents, barriers to her happiness. Their interventions in her courtship had only elicited anger and frustration.

"She won't listen to you," Olivia said. "But she might listen to Mr. Ringwell."

Chapter Twenty-Eight

S NEAKING UP TO the house where Dawson had stashed Constance proved easier for Thel, especially with Mr. Ringwell and Mr. Smith distracting the guards. The first board Thel pried away revealed a room full of stolen goods. He recognized several items from his own house that had gone missing. Although he'd been searching for his daughter, he was relieved to find he'd not lied to Constable Smith. He carefully pushed the board back into place and crept along the brambles surrounding the house until he reached the next window. This time, when he peered between the spaces, he saw his daughter.

She was sitting on the mangled remains of a couch, her arms wrapped around herself. She wasn't crying, but neither did she appear happy. He clenched the neck of the hammer in the hand not pressed to the window.

The temptation to smash open the window and ferry his daughter to freedom was strong, but he steeled himself. Olivia was right. If they acted in haste, Constance might refuse to leave. He'd assumed the awful state of her room meant she hadn't left willingly, but the mess might also have been the product of hasty packing. Mr. Ringwell had a better chance of convincing her she was making a mistake.

That didn't mean he had to like it.

If their plan fell to pieces, he was ready to barge in and confront Dawson. No one would stop him from getting Constance away.

"He is on the way," Olivia said as she crawled up beside him.

Thel thumped against the wall and closed his eyes. "What if it doesn't work?"

Olivia leaned beside him, pressing her side against his, without touching him directly. It was what she did, being present without interfering. He tucked his arm around her shoulders and pulled her close. That was where he wanted her, forever at his side.

The distant sound of horse hooves on gravel reached him, and he tensed. That would be Mr. Ringwell and the constable. Right on time. Constance rushed to the door and banged on it with her fists until it flew open.

She stumbled back as four men entered, Dawson in the lead, Mr. Ringwell close behind him, and then the constable.

Constance stood apart, as if she was unsure to whom she wanted to run. "What are you doing here, Mr. Ringwell?"

Dawson rushed to Constance, placing himself between her and the other men, but she quickly maneuvered out from behind him and inched closer to Mr. Ringwell.

"You shouldn't have come," Constance whispered.

"I couldn't let him do this to you," Mr. Ringwell said.

Constance wrinkled her nose. "Well, I didn't—"

"She is here of her own volition!" Dawson shouted. "We are to be wed tomorrow."

"Perhaps we should discuss this rationally," the constable said. "I would like to speak to each of you individually. Mr. Dawson?"

The man looked as if he were going to complain, but faced with the constable, he grumbled and left the room.

Exactly as they had planned.

The moment the door closed, Mr. Ringwell approached Constance. There was an awareness between them that had not been there before. It was as if the veil of Dawson's influence had been yanked away and Constance was seeing the world clearly for the first time.

Thel led Olivia away from their post and they entered the house from the front door the constable had left open for them. They had to leave it to Mr. Ringwell to convince Constance she was making a mistake. If he couldn't convince her, then everything was lost. Even if Constable Smith arrested Dawson for burglary, she would return to him the moment he got free. Knowing Dawson, he would not be behind bars long.

"Did you see her face when he came barging through the door?" Olivia giggled. "She's finally seeing what he has seen all these years. I think she loved him all this time, but she wouldn't let herself feel it." She sighed. "I know what that feels like."

He winced at the reminder. Of everyone in the house, Olivia understood the most what it was like to be blinded by love.

"I'm sorry that I didn't trust you," he said. If he had listened to her from the beginning, none of what had happened might have occurred. He had been too stubborn and set in his ways. He should have realized what had been happening under his own roof. In attempting to keep his family together, he had asserted his desires over them, exactly as he had promised he would not.

Olivia pressed her cheek to his chest. "I forgive you."

The sound of footfalls had her stepping back, and then Constable Smith returned, with Dawson in quick pursuit. For the first time, Thel saw fear on the man's face.

"Where is she?" Dawson asked.

"Still inside," Olivia said. "I would knock before you enter."

Dawson paled. "You left them alone together?"

Thel shrugged. "They have been friends since they were children. If I cannot trust him, I cannot trust anyone."

Dawson flung the door open.

Thel stayed where he was and couldn't help the smile that formed on his face when he heard Dawson's hiss of indrawn breath.

Olivia left his side and called, "Constance, are you ready to leave?"

"You can't!" Dawson said. He opened and closed his mouth a few times, then his face softened. "Connie. Darling. I've done so much for you. Are you really going to leave me now?"

Constance looked conflicted, but Mr. Ringwell tightened his arm around her. "Your tricks will not work on her anymore."

Dawson bared his teeth. "You will never have her. I have taken her. She is mine. We will be married, and I will have her dowry as my own."

Constance trembled. "What do you mean? John, I thought you said you didn't need my dowry. You said—"

"Cease your chatter, girl!" He spun and drew back his hand, as if to strike her, but Mr. Ringwell yanked her out of the way.

Her eyes filled with tears. "Why are you doing this?"

"Tell her what you've done," Thel said. "Or perhaps we should show you. Mr. Ringwell, bring Constance. Constable, there's something you'll want to see."

Against Dawson's complaints, Thel led them through the house until they reached the room where Dawson had stashed everything he had stolen. There were stacks of paintings on the floor, overturned bags of coins, and more jewelry than Olivia had ever seen in one place in her life.

Constance stepped inside and picked up a gold statue of a Pegasus with an ivory horn and diamonds for eyes. "This belongs to Lady Cowper. She said she lost it." Constance clutched the statue to her chest and whirled on Dawson. "You never loved me, did you? Lady Allen was right. You were just using me." She put her face in her hands. "I can't believe I was so stupid."

"Mr. Ringwell, take her outside," Thel said. "Mr. Smith, I believe you'll find this room contains many of the stolen items you have been searching for. In addition, Dawson kidnapped my daughter."

"Would you testify as such?" The constable looked at Olivia. "Both of you?"

"Yes," Olivia and Constance said at the same time.

The constable removed a pair of iron shackles from his pocket. "That is evidence enough for me."

Chapter Twenty-Nine

AFTER CONSTABLE SMITH had left with Dawson, Olivia found Mr. Ringwell holding a sobbing Constance in his arms.

"It is worse than we thought," Thel said. He looked even more grim than she felt. "We cannot be certain if she was seen leaving London with Dawson. If she was, and we do not return with news of a wedding, she will be ruined."

Constance sobbed harder. Mr. Ringwell clutched her close. "I won't let her return in disgrace. I'll marry her. No one will know that it was Dawson in the carriage instead of me."

The past was repeating itself, except it was Constance in Olivia's shoes. How had she let this happen? She wanted to scream and pound her fists on the ground. Constance was still a child, despite what society might think.

She pushed away from Mr. Ringwell and stood, trembling, before her father. "I will bear whatever shame I must. You've done enough for me, Father." Her eyes got watery again. "And Sam—Mr. Ringwell has sacrificed enough. I've made this mistake. I won't let others suffer because of it."

It truly seemed that they were left in an impossible position. Either Constance would marry and become a bride far too soon, or they would return to London, and she would have to weather the scandal of whatever society decided she had done.

An idea wormed its way into Olivia's head. Society knew they had gone missing, but they didn't know why. If they provided an even more salacious story, it might put them off the scent. Especially if it was at their own expense.

"There will still be a marriage today," Olivia said.

Constance screwed up her face.

Mr. Ringwell straightened his jacket. "I'm ready."

She smiled, letting some of Lady Allen enter her voice. "Oh, no. It is not you and Constance who will marry."

"Who, then?" Thel asked.

She raised her hand, and he took it, stepping closer until there was barely enough room between them for a book to fit. "I know this isn't what you intended when you asked me to marry you, but I'm willing to marry you now if it saves Constance."

Thel grimaced. "I have no ring, nor flowers. My parents and brothers are not here to witness our union. You aren't even wearing a wedding dress."

Olivia shook her head. "I've been through all of that before." Her wedding had been straight out of a fairy tale, everything her youthful self had desired. "If it helps Constance, then I can do without any of it."

Thel looked at Mr. Ringwell. "Do you still have the item you intended to use to propose?"

Mr. Ringwell patted his pockets, then handed over a slightly crushed circle of grass.

Constance gasped. "Is that what I think it is?" She put her hands over her mouth. "Oh, Sammy, you really do love me like that?"

Mr. Ringwell scratched the back of his neck. "It's nothing fancy, Connie. You deserve much better."

As Mr. Ringwell wrapped his arms around Constance, Olivia slid the ring on her finger and tucked it into place, then admired it. It was not the ornate gold band that the earl had presented her with. It was far more beautiful. Her imagination transformed the strands into braided silver.

He frowned. "I will buy you something more appropriate."

She plucked her hand back. "Perhaps later, but this will suffice for today. It is lovely, is it not?"

He smiled. "Yes, it is." Then his smile fell. "I suppose I should write to my family."

Olivia cringed. The thought of summoning them so far into the countryside when the season was not yet over made her feel like she was impinging upon their freedom and happiness. But Thel was right. It would lend additional weight to their story if they were all seen leaving town.

"I suppose we'll need to head to Gretna Green, after all," Olivia said.

"No need," Thel said. He removed a sheet of paper from his pocket and handed it to Olivia. "I applied for a special license weeks ago, before I asked you to marry me the first time."

She ran her fingers over the parchment. "You've held on to it all this time?"

He grinned. "Perhaps a part of me could not admit that what I did was wrong." Then he took her hands and his smile fell. "You are certain?"

Olivia squeezed his fingers. "I am."

❧

LATER THAT DAY, after a carriage ride through the country and a brief stop at the nearest church, they arrived at Thel's childhood home. Constance had not said a word throughout the trip. Mr. Ringwell clutched her hand.

She could not blame him. If they were alone, she would have crawled into Thel's lap and rested against his chest. She feared their plan would not work, but worse than that, she feared Constance would not recover from what she had been through. The shadows on her face were a painful reminder of Olivia's own trauma.

"We're here," Thel said.

She peered out the window as they passed through wrought-iron gates and started up the long path toward the house. A wide expanse of manicured gardens surrounded them on either side. A fountain stood outside the front entrance, depicting a willowy woman with flowing hair covering her like clothing.

"Home," Constance said, in a breathy voice. It was the first time she had spoken since they had entered the carriage, and Olivia was pleased to see some of the fear and worry erased from her face.

She did not relish the thought of how much work was ahead of her. She would have to rally the staff, prepare all the rooms for Thel's family, while adjusting to her new position.

Thel reached across the carriage and squeezed her knee. "We will do this."

That was the only part of the plan that she did not doubt in the slightest. She could not regret marrying him. She looked forward to presenting herself as not the Countess Dowager Allen, but as the Marchioness of Lowell, and one day, the Duchess of Hestia.

She would be a duchess.

Goodness.

She wished she could be an invisible observer in the room when Mrs. Zephyr and the other ladies who had spurned her learned of her marriage. Just imagining Mrs. Zephyr paling and sputtering was enough to make Olivia smile.

The carriage stopped. Thel opened the door, helped everyone inside exit, and then instructed the driver to park. Before they could enter the house, however, the doors flew open, and a woman dressed in a pale-blue day dress raced toward them.

"Celina!" Thel said. "What are you doing here?" There was no anger in his voice, only surprise, for which Olivia was grateful. She did not want to cause any further conflict.

Celina captured Constance in a hug. "Oh, I was hoping you would come here. It's not too late, is it? Please tell me you have not married him." She pulled back and looked around. "Where is Dawson?"

Mr. Ringwell grasped Constance's shoulder and gave the girl a look that was full of love. "That is a long story."

Constance's cheeks grew rosy. She touched Mr. Ringwell's hand with her fingers and dropped her gaze to the ground.

Olivia stepped closer to Celina, hardly recognizing her from the mean-spirited viper who had accused her of murder. What had changed since she had left Celina in that bedroom? Apparently, whatever it had been, it had been for the best. Then the meaning of Celina's words struck her. She'd known they'd been coming.

"Olivia, it is such a pleasure to see you again," Celina said as she took Olivia's hands. "I apologize for presuming, but when I learned what Mr. Dawson had done, I knew I had to try to stop him."

"How'd you know to come here? Did Lord Felix come with you?" Olivia asked. She was bursting with questions, but those were the most important.

"Oh, certainly not," Celina said. "After I told him of the affair, my husband ran off somewhere. Probably to drink himself senseless." She waved a hand in the air. "The man is terribly predictable. He'll sulk for a few weeks before crawling back to beg forgiveness. As to how I knew to come here, Constance told me."

Constance slapped a hand over her mouth, her eyes wide. "Oh, I forgot," she said, the words muffled by her hand.

"Constance," Thel said, in a tired voice. "What have you done?"

"I told Celina that we would honeymoon here. Me and Dawson." She flushed. "There is a lot we have to tell you, Aunt."

Celina drew herself upright. "I see. Come, I have arranged for afternoon tea. All of you look quite famished."

Chapter Thirty

THE HOUSE WAS quiet as Olivia walked toward the room where she would spend her first night as Lady Lowell. Unexpected nerves fluttered in her stomach. They'd had sex several times, but there had always been the edge of worry that someone would discover what they'd been doing. Would it be the same now that they were married?

Thel pressed a door open with his palm, and the sight that awaited her made her gasp. There were lit candles scattered across the room, and a copper tub near the hearth, filled with gently steaming water.

She was so shocked that she didn't realize Thel was moving forward until he tugged her hand. She followed, skipping to catch up. "Did you plan all of this?" she asked.

"Of course," he said. He tugged his cravat free, unwound it into a strip, then looped it around her neck and reeled her in. Their kiss was gentle at first, but soon they were both panting. She reached between their bodies and pressed her palm over the hard length of him, making him groan.

"Not tonight," he said. "Tonight, I want to cherish every second."

She unbuttoned his jacket, tugged his shirt free, then slid her hands beneath it. "As you wish. Show your mentor what you've learned."

He pushed her back until her knees knocked against the

bedframe. They tumbled down, laughing and kissing until she remembered the bath.

"Our water will grow cold," she said.

He rose above her on his elbows, his eyes dark and unreadable. "Disrobe."

A thrill passed through her at the command in his tone. This was a side of Thel she had never seen before.

She liked it.

At the same time, her contrary nature compelled her to disobey, even in a small way. She wanted to see what he would do if she was not the perfect, obedient wife.

She sauntered over to the bath and leaned over, thrusting her rear into the air. Then she reached down and slipped off her right slipper. She propped her foot on the edge of the tub and drew her hands up her thigh to the ties of her stockings.

❧❀❧

How was she driving him so wild when she was still fully dressed? He was hard as a rock, and her every movement was slow and seductive. She glanced up at him through her lashes, then flicked her tongue across her bottom lip. She hooked her thumbs beneath a stocking and slid it down until it gathered around her ankle.

"The water will be cold before you are done," he said. He wanted to step forward and tear the gown from her body, then shove his face into her breasts and scrape his teeth along her skin until that soft mewl came from her lips.

She took the tip of her gloved finger in her teeth and drew it off with half-lidded eyes, then did the same with the other. Her bare arms were a remarkable sight, such a simple thing, but enough to bring his cock to full attention.

She reached behind her back, did a little hop, then pouted. "I can't remove my gown."

He crossed the room and turned her so her back was to him, then untied the strings holding the gown on her body. When the bodice gaped, he smoothed his hand over her skin, then grasped the back of her neck and squeezed.

She grasped the sides of the tub. The water was quickly cooling, but he didn't care. He would summon another footman to bring buckets of boiling water once Olivia had the infernal gown and other garments off. He would shuffle her behind the curtains if he had to.

He finished untying the gown and separated the edges until she could step out. An enormous number of petticoats came next, followed by a crinoline. His hands moved with increasing speed and lack of grace as he peeled each layer away from her, revealing more of her delectable skin.

At last, he untied her corset strings and shimmied the garment over her head, leaving her wearing only her underthings and jewelry.

She bent down, craftily pressing her rear into his crotch as she removed her drawers and chemise, until she stood before him without an inch of fabric, one hip cocked, her hair still piled on top of her head.

His eyes flew to the apex of her thighs, where the triangular thatch of hair hid a bounty of pleasures.

"My earrings," she said, raising one hand to her neck, and the golden baubles hanging from her delicate lobes. He could not resist the taunt. He reached around and cupped her breasts in his hands, making her arch against him with a gasp. He kissed behind her ear, then took the earring and earlobe in his mouth. The slight metallic taste and the prong poking against the inside of his cheek should have been awkward, but it sent another throb of heat through him. He sucked gently, enough to make her gasp, then released his lips. He was tempted to tell her to keep them on—there was a particular flavor to having her still coiffed for the wedding from the neck up, but he did not want her to injure herself while they rolled around on the bed.

He removed her earrings one at a time, then tucked them into his pocket. Her necklace came next. As he unlatched it, he pressed wet kisses to her spine. Small tendrils of hair tickled his nose as the string of pearls went into his pocket with the earrings.

She writhed against him like a siren, shuddering as if he were already seated inside her. She reached up and touched the side of his head. He captured her hand and pressed a kiss to her palm.

She grasped her nape with her other hand. He captured it and raised her arms above her head.

He saw the lust in her reflection in the water, the flush of her chest, the rosy pink of her nipples. Her knees were pressed together, feet a foot or so far apart. He gathered both of her hands into one of his, then lowered his other hand to her stomach, splaying his fingers and pressing her against him.

"More," she whispered.

He inched his fingers down until he touched the crinkly hair outside her sex. She squirmed against him, but he held her hands tighter. He traced her outer lips with his thumb, up and down until she closed her eyes and breathed out shakily. Then he gently separated the folds and rubbed her clitoris in the manner she had shown him. Her hips rocked with his movement, bumping his crotch and sending jolts of pleasure through his cock. He pressed the tip of one finger inside her. She was so wet that there was no resistance. Her essence leaked onto his palm and dripped down his wrist. He added a second finger. She moaned and thrashed her head.

He could stand it no more. He released her hands to free his throbbing cock from his trousers, then pushed her forward with one hand until she was bent over the tub, her breasts dangling over the now-chilly water. He nudged her legs apart with his knee and took his cock in one hand, stroking himself from head to shaft twice. The tension in him grew that much sharper when she arched her back, lifting her rear for him. He grasped her hip with one hand and guided himself into her with the other. Once the head of his cock was inside, he savored the tightness of her before sliding deep.

The sound she made as he entered her frayed the already thin threads of his control, but he was determined not to spend himself too quickly. He began a slow, methodical motion, drawing himself almost completely out of her and then thrusting back inside in a powerful motion. The wet slap of their bodies drove him that much closer to release.

But he knew from their previous couplings that she would not find her pleasure this way. He wanted her to shudder around him before he filled her, have her contractions milk the seed from his cock.

As he was considering the logistics of providing her with additional stimulation, she reached around and pressed her middle finger to her other entrance. "Here."

He stilled and ran his thumb over the spot. "Are you certain? It is not as… lubricated."

"Watch." She coated her fingers in saliva before returning it to her arse.

He pulled out to give her room, but also because the sight of her inserting her fingers made him so hard that he had to squeeze his muscles to keep from spending himself.

A familiar fluttering around his cock alerted him she was close, and then she cried out and shuddered. It did not take long before he joined her, spilling himself into her as pleasure rocked through him and made his knees weak.

When her spasms ebbed, he slipped out of her and then gathered her into his arms and carried her to the bed. They were both sweaty and boneless with exertion, but he could not work up the energy to summon hot water.

They curled beneath the blankets, and he gathered her against him. She did not resist, but instead sighed as she rested her head on his chest and threw her leg over his. His cock twitched, but her gentle breaths and stillness suggested she was already asleep.

He settled back into the bed, certain that there was nowhere else he wanted to be.

Chapter Thirty-One

Six months later

O LIVIA LIFTED THE broom and tapped it on Constance's head. "You *do* have a gown, my dear."

Constance twirled, causing her glittering skirts to whirl around her. It was easy to imagine her as the forgotten stepchild of an uncaring family, granted a second chance by a magical, fairy godmother.

Olivia was more than willing to fill that role.

Constance stopped and thumped down on her bed, still grinning.

"Dizzy?" Olivia asked.

Constance settled her skirts and raised her chin. "It is simply the heat, my lady. I dare say it is stifling in this ballroom."

A laugh bubbled up Olivia's throat. Constance was an endless delight. Her mood had lifted considerably over the past few months. She had even allowed Mr. Ringwell to court her, although Thel insisted she wait until she was twenty before they married.

Mrs. Quill hovered in the corner, her hands at her waist, disapproval written across her features. Olivia had suggested they find a new employer for the stern woman, but Constance would have nothing of it.

"Mrs. Quill may be stern, but she can also be kind," Constance had said. So the woman remained, radiating disapproval every time Olivia and Constance engaged in their play.

Olivia set down the broom and sat beside Constance on the bed. "Are you looking forward to your reintroduction to society?"

Mr. Ringwell would be there, and so would many members of the Vaith household. It had taken weeks of negotiating for Thel to broker peace between his family, but everyone had eventually come around to the idea of another season for Constance, although they were all keeping a close eye on her after what had happened. Thel had even pulled Mr. Ringwell aside and instructed him not to ask Constance to marry him again until the end of the season, so that she could take things slowly. When Constance learned of this, she had not been so pleased, but neither had she complained. Perhaps she sensed the worry and relief that her uncles felt. Regardless, it made it difficult for Olivia to find time with her husband where they were not being observed.

At least they had their nights together.

A grin tugged on her lips. Thel was an eager learner, plumbing the depths of her knowledge, pushing her to the edge of her comfort, but no further. They had reached heights of pleasure that she had never thought possible. But more important than that, she felt she could truly be herself around him. She laughed hysterically when he tickled her sides, prancing around their room on her tiptoes when she was happy and even singing phrases of her favorite songs. Thel never shushed her. Sometimes he even joined in. The cruel streak she had feared he possessed had never appeared, and she had finally stopped waiting for him to change.

She touched her stomach. It was too soon to tell, but she suspected that there was a life growing in her. The dream that she had thought was dead had revived, and she couldn't wait for the day she held her child in her arms.

She still maintained her flirtatious act in public, but she felt more and more comfortable releasing it when she was around her friends and family. Thel's family had folded her into their flock as if she were any other of their relatives, and she felt blessed every time they sat down to dinner as a family. Thel had even forgiven Felix, although he had convinced the man to allow Celina to leave London.

A rap at the door had them both turning. Mrs. Quill answered it, then stepped aside as Thel entered, wearing a black suit. Olivia rose to meet her husband, holding her hands so he could take them. He smiled, and as usual, the way his eyes crinkled at the edges made her heart warm.

He leaned over and kissed her softly, eliciting a giggle from Constance and a sniff from Mrs. Quill.

"Are you ready, my love?" he asked.

She draped her arms over his shoulders. "Ready for what?"

He withdrew a wooden spoon from his jacket. "Ready to defend yourself!"

Constance squealed as he chased them around the room. Even Mrs. Quill unbent enough to smile. When Thel admitted defeat, he collapsed on the bed with a dramatic cry. Olivia and Constance joined him, bundled together like a warren of rabbits. Only months ago, Olivia would not have seen the value in such emotional closeness, but she'd learned much about herself since the first article had been published. She'd used matchmaking to fill a void in her life, occupying her time so she never had to confront her loneliness. Such a life no longer appealed to her.

She'd discovered something much better: a man who loved her, and whom she loved desperately in return.

THE END

About the Author

Melissa lives in Regina, Saskatchewan; the capital city that feels like a small town. A passionate public speaker, board game enthusiast, and lover of all things Halloween, she spends her free time writing and spoiling her two cats.

Website –
melissakendall.ca

Amazon –
amazon.ca/stores/author/B0B8JVQKMC

Facebook –
facebook.com/MAKendallAuthor

Instagram –
instagram.com/makendallauthor

X (Twitter) –
twitter.com/MAKendallAuthor

TikTok –
tiktok.com/@makendallauthor

Printed in the USA
CPSIA information can be obtained
at www.ICGtesting.com
LVHW022048221124
797277LV00003B/520